CHAPTER ONE

Telekinesis, the mental ability to manipulate objects through no physical interaction. Whenever this is mentioned, the general consensus is that of fantastic adventures that centre around a strong hero, ready to do all that is morally necessary to defend the helpless. Or a tyrannical villain ruling all through might and fear. However, Dorian Black's reality stood far less simplistic; no matter how much he desired the contrary.

His day always began the same way, with the destruction of his alarm clock. Every morning at exactly eight AM it would send out a steady vibrating pulse, if only for a moment, before being pushed across the room and smashed against the wall opposite. This act was done by his subconscious, as was normal for most Drem'onor, or Drem for short. A powerful species born with a specific ability to each individual. Back in days gone by, both their anatomy and power would adapt to their environment without thought. As times changed however, so did the Drem; finalising on a more Humankind appearance. This along with the change to their ability, which moulded to suit their position in the new society. This also meant that the true power in not only Steelhaven but across Gaia, rested solely in the hands of Humankind.

Dorian lay there staring at his ceiling, unwilling to stir. His apprehension about getting up was more to do with his desire to be lazy on that day than anything else. He had never been a morning person, not during his time served in the military and definitely not since he retired. That day was unlike most however, as it was the day that he would help his friend finalise her dream. That thought did not keep him from moving too quickly; It was only when he remembered what would happen if he were late, did he finally start to move. With a long sigh, he outstretched his four-poster bed and made a quick gesture towards his kitchen, starting an already full kettle for his morning coffee. Shifting his weight to his left, he planted his feet firmly onto the shaggy carpet surrounding his bed, matting his toes into the wool, a small comfort that helped him wake up. It was only when a secondary burst of pulses from his broken alarm sounded, did he drive himself forward. Pushing himself sharply off his bed and walking over to his en suite bathroom, he waved his hand over the alarm as he passed, reconstructing it in an instant. He had always taken pride in the control over his ability, a rare gift among the Drem of Steelhaven and even less with his strength. This feat was achieved solely through his military service. Looking around his home however, you would not come to the conclusion that he had served at all. Whatever accolades he had been awarded, were hidden away in his attic. All bar one, a medal for sixteen years long service, which he kept in his bedside cabinet. Gathering dust and away from prying eyes, but still there beside him. As a former marine, the extent in which he could legally use his ability in public was severely limited. So, when he was out amongst the general population, he would have to go out of his way not to use his power. In contrast to this, he expressed himself fully in private, a luxury he took great satisfaction from. As he walked into his bathroom, his sink began to fill with piping hot water, which was blocked from the drain with his power. Meeting the basin and looking into the bathroom mirror ahead, he pushed his electric shaver and wide toothed comb up off the shelf underneath to begin his morning routine. You can take the man out the army, but you cannot take the army out of the man. At least that was always his excuse as to why he kept such a close eye for any hair out of place. His short-undercut hairstyle, with the top having just enough hair to run his hand through. This along with his long, greying beard and even his eyebrows, had to be kept to an acceptable standard. As the appliances flew around his face, he turned to the fogged up secondary circular mirror to his left and began to set out his appointments for the day.

    09:00 Gym
    12:00 Suit shopping
    14:00 Lexa
    18:00 Fight
    23:00 Home

He then double checked the results of his morning clean up in the main mirror. Predominately to be sure that the fracture lines across his jaw were still hidden. They had come about through a basic training 'accident', at least that's what the official statement read. The truth of the matter was, it was a lesson. One that he would not forget. He absent-mindedly rubbed the index and middle finger of his right hand across his chin and up to his right ear reminiscing on that moment, that pain. Reminding himself never to be caught off guard like that again. Although covered, his jawline shown powerfully through his beard. This, coupled with his strong and high cheekbones, gaunt cheeks and bright emerald eyes, made him radiant a regal demeanor. This added to his reputation of being a hero to the masses. Although if they could see the true damage that the Steelhaven/Verthollow war had left on him, not just to his body, but to his mind. Then that status would vanish in an instant, as he wished it would. As he wiped away his schedule, he passively nodded to his reflection and turned to enter his shower.

Walking back into his bedroom feeling refreshed, his subconscious continued to push forward to get him ready, opening his wardrobe and pulling his gym clothes to him. As he was hovering in the middle of his bedroom and tightening the rope in his jogging bottoms, the doorbell rang. Without looking up, he gestured with his left hand through the open bedroom door and towards the intercom. "Yes?" He shouted from across the room, not welcoming the interruption in the slightest.

"Erm..." a nervous squeak replied. "Mr Black, I have your grocery order here, I... I hope I'm not interrupting." Dorian dropped to the floor, pulling his tank top straight as his feet slammed into the ground. He quickly marched over and snapped the door open. The teenage boy in front of him staggered back in alarm, dropping the tablet in his hand, which was easily caught by Dorian and pulled it up to his eye level.

"Morning." Dorian stated gruffly, impatient as he examined the list. After an awkward silence passed between the pair, Dorian remembered his manners and greeted the boy again, giving the tablet back as he did so. "Good morning Tom, I hope everything is in order. How is school going? You are studying Product Management if I'm remembering correctly." He questioned in a politer tone. The boy nodded back, looking down at the ground to miss Dorian's gaze. With a few shaky taps on his tablet, he twisted the device back for Dorian to sign.

"It's going well thank you." He wheezes under his breath, trying to calm himself. "I... I'm having a little trouble with a couple of the assignments, but I should be able to get them finished on time."

"I'm glad to hear it." Dorian stated, getting a small smile out of the boy. "Good luck kid, let me know how you get on." Dorian replied pulling the box of largely fruit and vegetables up to his hands. With a nervous smile, the courier bowed and in a sharp pillar of bright light, he was gone, leaving Dorian to retreat back into his home.

It was only a five-minute walk to the twenty-four-hour gym around the corner. So, after pushing his shopping away and grabbing his gym bag, which contained his suit for the meeting after his workout. Dorian took the short walk over, pushing his door locked as he left. As soon as he entered, he was greeted not only by the loud music but also by the only pair that would be there so early on a Sunday. Elizabeth and Jack, the gym addicted couple spotting each other over on a cable machine just opposite the main entrance. Both in their early twenties, with bodies that looked like they had spent at least half of their lives in the gym. Jack casually nodded in Dorian's direction as he passed them by, Elizabeth was too focused on her set to react. Dorian returned the welcome with a wave as he walked over to the treadmills that lined the back wall. Plastered above him were inspirational quotes to encourage those inside to push themselves. Dorian put on his headphones to focused on his music as he ran, but only to a point, as not focusing on his power would make things happen without his intention. The last example of this happened a year ago.

It was eleven o'clock at night and Dorian had just left his parttime, cash in hand job as a cleaner at Revelations, a high-end gourmet restaurant that focused on overpriced 'healthy' food. Even though his military pension was more than enough to cover all his expenses, he did not like to sit idle for too long. Strolling down the street, the autumn winds blew hard around him, which he worked to his advantage, as he could use his ability to aid in pushing over things littering the street, which was always a source of entertainment. As a recycling bin threw to the ground, throwing the plastic bottles down an alleyway to his right. His gaze was pulled to see a small group fighting, on instinct, Dorian slowly walked toward them. Huddled together were two women, one defending the other from a group of six Omegans. A 'political' group of Humankind who, above all else, hated the Drem, feeling as though they were the cause for all Steelhaven's problems. The two victims were in their early twenties. The young girl on her feet was defending herself quite well, her Bo staff connecting hard and precisely against her attackers. However, with their superior numbers, they were continually getting cross shots in. So, when Dorian had gotten a few feet away from them, the woman had buckled onto one knee, still trying her hardest to stay in the fight. Forgetting himself, he stepped out of the shadows and shouted, projecting his voice as loud and as far as he could. "Enough!" his power pushed all the attackers off their feet, while protecting the two women on the ground in a small domed shield. One of the attackers hit the side of a car parked far off on the other entrance of the alley, breaking both windows on the passengers side on impact. Dorian dragged the defenceless attackers to a corner to his right and walked to those he went to help. Thinking he was another attacker, the woman spun around and swung her staff towards Dorian's face. It took little effort to hold her attack in check. Fear rushed through her, right down to her bones; this fear was quickly settled by Dorian with a smile and an out stretched hand to introduce himself. That was also the day when he met Alexandra O'hearn or Lexa as he would come to call her.

Finishing off his ten-minute jog, Dorian let the last track of the treadmill push him off. Such a short run wouldn't normally be enough of a workout for most people. However, it was just enough for him, as he subtlety used his power to push his body into full contraction, allowing a complete working of the related muscles. Dorian panted slightly as he walked over to the water fountain next to the changing rooms. On his way over, he looked to the main entrance to see Lexa walk in. An imposing woman, just passing six-foot-tall with a solid build of muscle on her frame. Long, bright auburn hair was pulled back into a ponytail, which amplified her cheekbones and fullness of face. Noticing Dorian's gaze, she smiled and walked over.

"Hey Dor, you're not normally here this early, what gives?" Lexa asked, already knowing the answer. "Trying to run away from the inevitable call of death?"

"My groceries arrived early, so I had time to spare, go warm up and I'll set everything out." Dorian responded, ignoring the jab at his age. Instead, he reached out a hand to greet her properly. Lexa's smile widened as she pushed his greeting aside and gave him a big hug instead, then sharply brushed passed before he could object. Watching as Lexa walked over to greet Elizabeth and Jack with another surprise hug, Dorian went over the training routine he would put her through today. He was a lot stricter on her training than anyone else that he had trained, even harder than on himself. This was partly because of the large sense of responsibility that he felt over her. After their first meeting, Dorian had helped Lexa push through her issues and she, in turn, helped Dorian become more acclimatized to civilian life. They both agreed to stay in contact. This eventually grew into a friendship. After the first few months, Lexa finally collected enough courage together to ask him to train her just like he had been. He hesitated at first, especially how they met. It was only after her second run in with a fight, the one that kept her secret safe that he began to trust her enough. Just like what he did for himself, Dorian used his power to push Lexa further past her limit, a little further every day. Today was chest and shoulders before going back to the studio. That was where the personal trainers at the gym would hold the official gym classes. Dorian used the same space to do some of their usual combat training. Dorian and Lexa had learned several different fighting techniques from over a dozen different martial arts, focusing primarily on quick strikes with strong guards.

Before leaving the gym, Dorian marched from the studio, directly over to the men's changing rooms. As Lexa realised where he was going, she sighed to herself, not for him changing into fresh clothes. At herself, for again forgetting to bring her own. With the power to control memories, it was especially frustrating for her whenever she forgot something. The upbeat music that was blasted in the gym was suddenly replaced by a news report. Within the broadcast, the reporter stated that the conflict continues over in the farming district. Both terror attacks done by the Omegans and another extremist group named the Nephilim, the latter being made up solely of Drem. The fight had begun over several days ago and any intervention by the police made no effect at stopping it. Hearing this news infuriated Lexa, empowering her resolve into following up with her plan to do something about it. Dorian took ten minutes to change his clothes, more than enough time for Lexa to calm herself down. With the attacks increasing over the past several months. Lexa would have heated debates with her mentor about the right course of action. After several of these disputes however, Dorian had gotten more and more frustrated as it felt to him that they had gotten as far as they could. This however, did not stop Lexa from being up the topic, simply because she enjoyed antagonising him.

After the ten minutes, Dorian walked out dressed in a dark green four-piece suit and military green overcoat, He continued passed Lexa and out the front door and down the street. Lexa could only wave politely at Elizabeth and Jack as she hurried after him, still in her faded violet gym attire and matching hoodie.

"Are you sure I can't convince you to get a suit for yourself? Together, we could finally show those extremist groups where they stand." Lexa probed as she playfully punched Dorian's arm. "I'll let that go considering that you haven't been on your first true run through yet." Dorian replied, quickening his pace to continue to push Lexa, which she found barely tolerable. "However," he continued, "...there is no glamour to this quote, unquote 'business', because it's technically not legal." Lexa laughed at this as the two are parted for a moment by a large crowd walking in the opposite direction.

"I'm sure this has nothing to do with those in charge asking you to go all political and kill a severely corrupt government official." Lexa finalised with a laugh, Dorian however, did not find her passing remark amusing and stopped her in her tracks. Grabbing Lexa's arm and using his ability to subtlety brush people aside, he stared at her menacingly.

"That has nothing to do with it. Do not talk about matters that you have no idea about, I would not and will not be a puppet, someone who would make the morally grey choice and be a scapegoat when things go wrong." His voice deepened slightly.

The small amount of rubbish that littered around them slowly lifted off the ground. The hairs on the back of Lexa's neck stood on end and she realised that she had pushed too far.
"I never meant anything bad by it, honest." Lexa tried to put her hand on his shoulder, however, she couldn't move a muscle. "I was just retelling the rumours from back then." The icy cold look held strong on Dorian's face and it took a while before it faded, he turned sharply on the spot and continued forward, with Lexa frozen behind. After a while the force passed away. Lexa stumbled forward. She steadied herself and rushed to catch up.

In the centre of Market District sat a towering marble rectangular pedestal, in the middle of an octagon shaped fountain. On top of the pedestal stood a statue of a mounted lancer, the front legs of the cavalier's horse are up in the air, signifying that he had died in combat. In the statue's right hand was an engraved flag. Stamped in the centre was the ancient symbol of the merchant families that had originally founded Steelhaven. Eight stars all in individual circles connected at a pivotal point at the centre. Symbolizing a six-sided set of weighing scales. As the pair got closer, Lexa watched as the outer rim of the fountain shoot fresh water towards the statue, cascading off the column and back down into circulation. When they got to the fountain's base, Dorian sat down by the water's edge, he then reached down and pressing his hand into the water, still not taking note of his friend. With a small pushed wave into the water, he found what he was looking for. "If I'm completely honest, I'm not sure if I'm ready for the next step." Lexa confessed as she sat down on his right side, her hands clasped together in her lap. "I thought I was ready before, but that clearly wasn't true." Dorian turned around in his seat, looking straight ahead. He rested his hand on her shoulder while revealing the item he had just acquired in the other. A small silver coin branded with the same symbol flying high above. On the other side of the coin were engraved three words, 'Power. Wisdom. Courage.' The country's motto. Lexa smiled at this, even though she had pushed too far with her words, that simple act of showing such a dangerous item in public, showed he wasn't really that mad. She nodded slightly as Dorian placed the coin the inner pocket of his overcoat.

"You can never truly be ready when it comes to this kind of work, there were times; now in hindsight that could have been handled better." Dorian's voice trailed off slightly, possibly reliving a painful mistake. After a moment of silence, he continued. "All you can do is prepare and react to any complications that arrive." With an empathetic look at each other, they stood up and Dorian began retelling a story about one of his operations.

CHAPTER TWO

"**...T**hey didn't give me much choose, neither side wanted to stand down." Dorian finalised as he opened up the door the shop door of Smith and Taylor, the best tailors in the city. Stopping her at the door, Dorian commanded "Remember to go for your measurements and let me sort out the rest, it's best to keep you separate from the manufacturers, we don't need a paper trail leading back to you." To which she nodded understandably. As she walked over to the fitting room just to the left of the main entrance, Lexa smiled politely at the cashier and walked through the beaded entrance. Before they both disappeared out of sight, Lexa watched as Dorian stepped over to the register and placed the silver coin in a charity box on the far left of the counter.
"Welcome to my shop, Ms O'hearn, it's a pleasure to finally make your acquaintance." Lexa's head bolted around to acknowledge who had greeted her, standing in a perfectly fitted maroon three-piece suit was the proprietor of the establishment, Olabode Taylor. A slender man in his mid-fifties, shinning bald head and a small, grey goatee protruding fiercely from his chin. His eyes were as black as charcoal, cold and unyielding. He strode over with vigour and presented a gloved hand to welcome his client. 'This is a man that takes himself far too seriously, better be nice.' Lexa thought to herself as she accepted his handshake. Olabode brought up his other hand and shook Lexa's right hand with both of his, taking a slight bow as he did so. Lexa however, was

far too entranced by her surroundings to give him her full attention. Filtering down from the ceiling, down to the edges of the silk carpet underfoot were dozens of coloured rolls of patterned fabric. Starting with red to her left, moving across to pink, purple, navy, green, blue and orange. With each new roll, the colours melding seamlessly across the spectrum, forming a shower of colour that moved lightly in the breeze from a small skylight in the centre of the room. The smell of incense overwhelmed the senses, a rich aroma of Lavender and jasmine. To the right side of the entrance, Lexa noted a freshly made pot of tea on top of a beautifully, hand crafted serving table; laced with a gold pattern throughout its base finished with a marble top. A shiver ran down Lexa's spine as she stepped onto the measuring stool in front of her, feeling a little out of place in such an upper-class establishment. Returning back to Mr Taylor, she nodded back to him with an artificial smile. Quickly releasing her hand, Mr Taylor lifted his right hand up and flamboyantly snapped his fingers. At that moment, two teenage girls in uniform moved silently in from the back room and bowed together in unison. Wearing pink suits similar to Mr Taylor, except they wore skirts. Awestruck by their sudden appearance, Lexa returned their greeting, it was only when she lifted her gaze to stand back up right, did Lexa notice the girl's white gloves. Throughout Steelhaven society and other cultures beyond, there was one fundamental indicator of law about restrained Drem, that being some form of brand identifying them as such. Some places, like Steelhaven itself, it was a tattoo which could be removed upon their release. However, considering the tattoo of Steelhaven's Drem was the white scorpion on their right thigh, Lexa knew something was wrong. She did all she could to stay calm, as Taylor's 'assistants' took her measurements. After several unanswered questions from Taylor, he looked at her with confusion before realising what was going on. With a heavy sigh, he turned and stormed out in frustration.

It did not take long for the two girls to take Lexa's measurements, as soon as they had finished, they tried to vanish away without making eye contact. Lexa grabbed both of their forearms and they instinctually drop to their knees. "It's okay, it's okay, you're not in trouble." Lexa reassured them as she helped them up. They both look at her puzzled, that swiftly changed to shock as Lexa tried to remove one of their gloves. The girl in question, on Lexa's right, tore away from her and stared in shock and clasped her hand held tightly to her chest. Lexa calmly turned her hand over, "Please" she requested kindly. The girl hesitated for a spell before placing her hand in Lexa's and dropping her head. Lexa rolled away a fraction of the glove down, just enough to confirm her suspicions. Layered on the back of the young girl's hand was a thick mound of callus skin, must have been from when her owner had tried to forcefully remove a mark. Lexa clenched her teeth in anger. They were imported slaves, she knew of several countries that scared their Drem, but without seeing that particular brand shape, she would not know which one. Grabbing the other girl's hand, she placed a fifty Konzar note into each of their hands. Lexa firmly held the two girls' hands as they frantically tried to return the money. "It's okay, I won't say anything." Lexa comforted they pair, uncertain how-to response, they just nodded softly.

"I Hope everything is going swimmingly in here" Taylor declared, striding back into the room. This caused the two girls to vanish on the spot. This peaked his interest and he stormed over to confront Lexa. "I hope you are not giving my employees any ideas, Ms O'hearn." The polite grace in his voice had dried up, leaving a sombre tone and sour expression on his face. Instead of the timid reaction that he was expecting, Lexa stepped off the stool she was standing on for her measurements and smiled broadly.

"Now Mr Taylor, whatever would give you that idea?" Lexa jested, looking down at the man, knowing he couldn't answer without giving himself away, his expression lightened slightly.

"Your suit will take two hours to complete, Mr Black is waiting for you at the front desk." He stepped back slowly and gestured towards the door, his kind demeanour recovering too slowly to be on show. Lexa laughed to herself as she passed through the beaded door.

Walking through the entrance so quickly, Lexa hadn't noticed the grandeur of shop's showroom. Red oak display cabinets across the wall in front of her, all of them housing extremely expensive and handmade suits, linking the main entrance with the main desk, a dark oak counter running the span of the back wall. Walking over, Lexa saw the impatience in Dorian's eyes and she smiled back. Alongside Dorian was the cashier, a small boy of about twelve or thirteen by Lexa's guess. With short curly Black hair and sour look on his face. He was wearing a light blue shirt, set under a deeper blue striped waistcoat. She shook the boy's hand, which surprised him and made him smile uneasily back, she noted the golden watch on his left wrist. Clearly dolled up to show a good impression to the customers. She made a point to continue the handshake as Taylor passed them. He looked at her with such contempt and scoffed as he walked into to his office and shutting the door firmly behind him, continuing that judgemental look at her until the door was fully shut. Lexa could barely keep herself from laughing again, with only a slight glance at Dorian's disapproval. "Why do you always have to enjoy creating conflict so much? I thought you would have grown out of that by now." Dorian calmly asked as he settled his part of the bill with an envelope full of money. With the exact amount written on the outside, along with his full name and the date of purchase. He then stepped slightly aside and away from the cashier and gestured for Lexa to do the same. Unlike Dorian's crisp notes, Lexa pulled out handfuls of dirty, torn and discoloured cash and dumped them on the table.

"I'm glad to disappoint." Lexa jested as she enveloped his payment with hers and smiled at both of them. Lexa often took pleasure in putting Dorian in social situations that made him uncomfortable, which was frequent. In her mind, it was all to help him be more at ease. Dorian sighed heavily, signed both his and the shop's receipts and passed their copy back; averting the cashier's displeasure of Lexa's act. She took notice of this and continued her smile. She slightly shrug signifying 'ah well, it happened,' she turned back to face Dorian. "So, what time am I meeting up with you again after this? I have lunch with Kimmi in half an hour." Lexa finished as she checked her inward facing watch, an anniversary gift from Kimberly, her girlfriend of four years and best friend for most of her life. "Considering the disorder of your schedule today, I'd say midnight?" she joked trying to coax an answer, adding a large display of her watch so Dorian could see. He, however, just finished his conversation with the cashier, apologising for her fleeting behaviour. The cashier had no interest in his apology and continued to scowl at Lexa. Without saying a word, Dorian grabbed Lexa's wrist firmly, pressing her watch down and moving them both over to the furthest glass display, next to the front entrance. Lexa pulled herself easily out of his grip and stepped back, this was not how Dorian would normally act.

"I will no longer tolerate these childish antics, not only do they draw unwanted attention..." Dorian exclaimed in a whisper, staring at her fiercely, his eyes as cold as his tone. "...But it will influence your attitude when you're out there." Dorian signified with a covert point outside. Lexa looked back in wonder, she understood what he meant, making light of a situation can cause compilations in the future, it was his mantra. A sudden wave of rage built inside Lexa however, wiping away her reason.

"Remember what you told me last month? When I turned to you for advice on what I should do to face down the intolerance in this city." Lexa argued back, her right hand clenching into a fist. She shifts up to stand up straight, so she looked down on him, her eyes now ablaze. "A person's actions are theirs alone, I can only teach you how to defend yourself." Lexa continued, mimicking Dorian's low speech pattern, slowing it further to mock. Stepping forward in frustration. "But ultimately, it is your judgement that weighs the most." In an eruption of anger, Lexa grabs Dorian by the throat, putting pressure in the right places to allow him to continue to talk but also so she could lift him a foot in the air. She pushed him back against the glass case, cracking it slightly. Dorian had never been much of a physical fighter, he let his power fight for him. This was the opposite for Lexa as her reach was severally limited in comparison. This also made her twice as strong physically. "Which means I will act however I please and I am damn sure that I do…not" her grasp tightens "…need your help." Dorian's temper rose to rival Lexa's, his eyes whitening slightly. He used his power to lock all the doors into the door, including Olabode's office door and the worker's entrance.

"Release me now!" Dorian roared, his calm and smooth voice lost to deep growl that spread to encase everything in his sight; using the vibration of that demand to insulate the room to keep anyone from hearing what was happening inside. With a firm push forward, Lexa pushed Dorian hard through the display case, destroying both it and the manikin inside. "Fine, have it your way." He continued, having gotten his answer, Dorian begun to deal with the last witness of the scene, the young cashier. Dorian cracked his neck away from Lexa's raised fist, which was fighting against Dorian's power so she could hit him across the face with enough force to break Dorian's jaw clean off. He slides his gaze across room and as he did, Dorian was meet with a strange sight. The boy was leant back in his wooden chair, his arms crossed and a broad smile on his face. In the split second before Dorian made the boy crash against the shelves behind him, Dorian noticed the similar tinge of white that had enveloped the boy's eyes. The boy's head cracked against the shelves and the sudden wave of hostility vanished as quickly as it had arrived.

The heat visible in Lexa's eye went and she placed Dorian gently back on the ground, apologising profusely. Dorian, unconcerned by her pleases for forgiveness, accepted one of them and marched over to the counter.

"No really Dor, I honestly don't know what came over me." Lexa continued following him to the counter. With a lift of his hand, Dorian dragged the child in the air and shook him awake. The boy's eyes splintered open to be met by Dorian's sharp look. His eyes had not only gone completely white, but the effect had crept across his face, causing his skin to turn marble, in stark contrast of his veins that had turned jet black. Reaching forward, Lexa tried to stop this attack, but Dorian held her back with ease.

"What did you do?" Dorian demanded as he outstretched and separated the boy's limbs. It was then that the simple fact hit Lexa, the sudden burst of rage, that was the boy's doing. Normally she would be the voice of reason, giving the boy a chance to explain himself, however she also wanted answers. She placed her hand on Dorian's shoulder interrupting him listening to the child's vague explanation. In silent agreement, Dorian pulled the boy toward him so Lexa could grab the boy's shoulder and learn all she could by using her own power. Finding out the truth by viewing his memories first hand, knowing that he could not lie.

Malik Taylor was his name and he had the power to control emotions. He had spent his entire life in servitude to his father, Olabode Taylor; like his mother Gianna before him. His mother had been a highly skilled seamstress, taught exclusively by Mr Taylor. Olabode held her in the highest regard over his other paid employees. She went into labour on the eleventh of September in the middle of the shop and had to be rushed to the hospital on the other side of the city. After forty-eight hours in labour, she finally gave birth at seven forty-two in the morning. The first few years of Malik's life went well, at four years old however, his mother died in an accident that Malik only heard from his father. With no details, as the whole ordeal left Olabode heartbroken. Olabode's heart had been with Gianna so when she dies, Olabode bore a fierce resentment towards Malik and refused to teach him the same skills given to his mother so openly. He fired all his paid employees and secretly brought Drem children in and hid them from public view. His resentment turned to hate over the years, which peaked on Malik's seventh birthday. Olabode had grown cruel, regularly beating the children in his employ, all but Malik who he could not bring himself to physically strike. This did not protect him from hearing the cries of those his father did hurt, at midnight on the night of his birthday Malik finally collected his courage and walked down into the slave quarters, to the end of the corridor and peaking through the door of the chamber of one of his friends, Darren. As soon as he saw the full extent of his father's barbarism, he bashed the door open to confront him. Darren was cowering in the corner, on top of his straw bed, his whole right side covered in blood and bruises. Olabode stood over him with a metal rod in his hand, holding it high above his head. As he heard the door swing open, he slowly turned around, a face of pure hate beamed through the blood.

"What do you think you're doing here boy? Get out!" Olabode screamed, gesturing with the metal rod towards the door, blood dripping off the end. "I said get out, before I do something you will regret." Olabode continued, walking towards his son. But Malik didn't move an inch.

"Please stop." Malik pleaded and in that moment, Malik wished with all his heart that his father would stop, to just see reason about what he was doing. To his surprise, he did just that, the anger snapped out of Olabode's face being replaced with an emotionless mask, the metal rod dropped to the floor. They both stared at each other for a moment with Malik's look in wonder at his father's glazed stare. Malik felt a strong prickle at the back of his head, a frost that struck him. Malik shivered and laughed at the chill. Then a low chuckle started from across the room. His father had begun to replicate Malik's laugh in his own monotone voice. That laugh grew louder and clearer until he began to convulse and twist with hysterics. His unnatural cackle echoed through the stone corridors of the underground caverns. Hearing the sounds from their own chambers, the other slaves walked towards the open door, one of them wise enough to pick up one of the flaming torches housed in the walls, Olabode cries had become hoarse by the point they had got close enough to see inside. Peering into the room, the light of the sickly green flame revealed the scene. Olabode's laugh had gone, he was instead clasping his throat in a desperate attempt to catch the breath that failed him. But it was no use, he collapsed onto the ground. The other children cheered wildly and break off. Half to help Darren and the other half to pick Malik up in celebration. They were so caught up in their excitement, that they did not notice that Malik had passed out with blood falling from his nose and eyes.

After receiving a firm nudge from Dorian to hurry up, Lexa sped through the rest of Malik's memories. She noted how the next five years, Malik used his power to help his friends acclimatise themselves to the servitude which puzzled her. So, when she was back in the present, she had to ask.

"If you had this power, why would you stay in servitude?" she questioned in a soft tone as she let him go. Pulling him out of Dorian's grasp and placing him on the ground. "Out of all the places to be you choose to stay here? And the rest of them, surely you could have gotten them all out." Concern swept across Lexa's face as she knelt down to speak to him. Straightening his clothes and steadying himself on the counter, Malik took his time to answer.

"That isn't your business." Malik eventually replied, trying to sound braver than he felt. Dorian crossed his arms just as Lexa reached out again to find out her own way. "Okay, okay." Malik panicked, holding his hand up. "I can change someone's emotion like nothing, but it got no effect on their minds." Malik started retelling a story of his childhood Lexa had not seen. How he tried to change his father's opinion and owning slaves, only to cause him to be happy or scared without any change in his opinion about the subject. At the end, Malik thought he had made some headway in changing his mind only to be stricken across the face. His father had explicitly forbidden him from ever using his power, especially on him. "So now what, are you going to go around spreading lies? You have just as much to hide as me." Malik retorted mockingly, his pride returning slowly.

At this, Lexa felt dumbstruck, in all the confusion she had not thought of a way of this situation that didn't make things worse. Her mind raced to find a solution and it showed on her face giving Malik large sense of satisfaction.

"I have nothing to hide, I fought for this country. Do you honestly think anyone would take your word over mine?" Dorian questioned, continuing before Malik could respond. "We will talk to your father about this, powers or not, it was still an unprovoked attack and that shall not go unpunished." Dorian addressed, unmoved by Malik's threat. Lexa looked at him in subdued awe, moments ago, they both had been under the thrall of this boy. If he wanted to play puppeteer again, the pair had little defence against it. Then it hit her, Malik had even said it himself, he could change people's emotions however he could not connect them to that person's morals. She smiled to herself happily that she had worked it all out but then saw the slight glance Dorian shoot her and to mimic his stance.

"Yeah kid, I don't think your father would appreciate you angering one of his most loyal customers." Lexa interjected. As she said this, Dorian begun to rescind the sound-proof bubble he had erected during the fight. "Regardless of what you tell him and even if he does believe you over us. Given the last twenty minutes, do you think we'd let you tell anyone else?" Lexa threatened with a little echoing of her own branching out. This must have caught Olabode's attention, because ruffling came from inside his office. Thankfully his desk rested on the other side of the room, so Dorian not only had time to completely remove the bubble surrounding them. He was also able to reconstruct the shelves behind Malik and the display that had gotten destroyed, if only for the time they needed to leave this situation. Dread swept through Malik when he heard the door open, swinging around to try and stop him talking to the pair. Before he could say a word, however, Dorian had already outstretched his hand out to grasp Olabode's firmly, a smile branded on his face. This surprised the entire group.

"Mr Black? I didn't realise you were still here, is there anything I can help you with?" Olabode questioned, his voice quivering at the end in surprise at Dorian's forwardness.

"As a matter of fact, there is good sir," Dorian declared shaking Olabode's hand firmly once more before letting go. "It comes to my attention that you have powered children under your employ. Imagine my surprise when hearing of this. I have been coming to your establishment for years, getting all my formal attire here and seeing none of this." Olabode sighed in what Lexa took as relief until he shot her a dirty look.

"I am very sorry you had to hear about that sir," he confessed as his eyes shifted slowly back from Lexa to Dorian. "But I can assure you that all the regulations of the Registration Agreement are being upheld. Article 8-C, which clearly states. 'All registered powered beings must learn a profession suitable for their ability and the betterment of the community. This includes those too young to complete their term of service and obtain their freedom.'" Reciting this so dully that Lexa knew that he must have memorised this speech for this very occasion. She went to respond, Dorian beat her to it.

"I understand that sir, I do not wish to cause an argument here. Where else would I get my suits from?" Dorian asked getting a slightly forced laugh from Olabode. "However, I wish to understand, why the secrecy? As you say, the law is on your side, so why not openly have your employees ready to help your customers with whatever they require?" The smile on Dorian's face made it difficult for Olabode to gauge his intent, his understanding on whether Dorian was expressing his approval or criticism on the subject was interrupted however by Malik's admission.

"They know about me, sir." Not only was this the first time Malik had spoken since his father and entered the room, but his inflexions had become much more rigid. Olabode turned around to look at his son. Fear rushing through him, whether that be fear of losing a son, or an employee, Lexa could not tell. He rested his hand on his son's shoulder, pulling him back slightly. Malik cowered on the spot, for all his posturing before, Lexa had not thought of the fear his father would imbue in his son.

"He means that we know your dirty little secret and you should be ashamed of how you have treated children!" Lexa yelled, grabbing Olabode's hand away from Malik. Her confrontation was cut short by Dorian, who separated them both with enough of a gap so that he could stand in between them and continue his conversation uninterrupted. He shot Lexa a stare before turning back.

"I can see why you're upset, I, however, we have no intention of going to the police. I had a different idea in mind. I wish to buy them off you. All of them." Dorian requested, looking down at Malik. Olabode distrusting posture stiffened at this request.

"Mr, Black, while I can understand your wish to help others with the same…affliction. I'm afraid that my indentured servants are not for sale." Olabode responded coldly brushing the sleeve of where Lexa had grabbed him. Feeling no need to hide his powers at that remark, Dorian pulled out the check book and pen out from the inner pocket of his overcoat, wrote his desired amount on one and passed it over to Olabode. He picked it out of the air and when he saw the amount, his stern expression fell to that of pure astonishment. He staggered back onto the chair at the front desk, his eyes wide and his right hand over his mouth trying to hold in a laugh of delight.

"Do…do you want them now? I can go get them now if you wish." Olabode spat fanatically snapping his gaze up. Knowing that would have changed his attitude, Dorian smiled again and takes his check sharply from Olabode's hand.

"Not so fast, I wish to inspect my purchases first." Olabode was on his feet, agreed whole heartedly and charged into the other room before Dorian could finish. As he watched Olabode leave, he turned to be greeted by Lexa, who was not pleased in the slightest.

"Your purchases? It sounds like you support what he's doing to these children." Lexa stepped forward and growled down to Dorian. "You honestly think this is right, slavery and child abuse? How can you give this man money? Basically, rewarding everything he has done to them." Dorian's eyes stared back at her, his expression unchanged.

"Trust me, he will get everything he deserves. Now I want you to go for your lunch with Kimberley. I will handle this and meet you in an hour and a half, alright?" He finalised placing his hand on her shoulder. Lexa took a deep breath in and nodded reluctantly.

"Okay, give me a call on how it goes."

"Of course," Dorian smiled and turned around to continue the matter at hand.

"See you later kid." Lexa shouted behind her on the way to the front door. There was no reply as Malik was dumbstruck about what had just happened.

CHAPTER THREE

"So, you just walked out? That's not like you at all." Kimberley asked, lifting a tall glass of white wine to her lips. Lexa smiled back happily, the light in her eyes beaming over at her girlfriend. That light had been there since the moment she had first meet Kimberley at the age of eight. When her father, a Pyromantic Colonel in the Imperial army, had moved her and her mother to the other side of the country as he had been put in charge of Thamon, the military base on the south coast. Kimberley's kindness and compassion in the difficult transfer to the new place was clear from the very beginning. It helped Lexa focus on her studies at school and not the bullies that harassed her. It also gave her the courage to express her true self, not just to her father and the rest of the world. But to the woman she knew that she wanted to spend the rest of her life with. Lexa pinched Kimberley's hand in playfulness.

"Hey now, I don't always have to be the one to finish a fight." she chirped back, letting go of Kimberley's hand to grab a roll of bread as they waited to order their meal. Kimberley just shoot back a knowing smile as she grabs her own bread. "Maybe some of the time, but I always know when to walk away." Lexa concluded.

"If only you'd had that mindset when that drunkard grabbed my bum in the club last week." Kimberley joked back.

"That was not my fault." Lexa countered, pointing her freshly broken bread across the table. "He should have known how to manage his drink, he was just lucky to get away with a broken nose"

"And his friends that came to help, did they deserve similar treatment? Granted, I didn't feel too bad about you defending my honour. The end results however, seemed ...excessive" Kimberley confessed, sipping the last of her wine.

"Maybe, although one did had Crystallokinesis, so they weren't completely defenceless, just outclassed."

"Good afternoon ladies, I hope everything is to your satisfaction thus far," said a polite voice from the right of their table. Lexa knew at once who it was, their usual waiter Dean, his uniform looked shabbier than the rest of the waiters. As Kimberley recited her and Lexa's main course, she smiled quietly to herself as she saw Dean leaning his small order pad on his thigh instead of the table. She taps the part of the table closest to him. "Thank you, Ms Sangster... Kimberley sorry." Dean said appreciatively in a laugh as he placed his serving tray upside down on the table, allowing him to slow his pace slightly and writing their orders more clearly.

"How's life as a new parent treating you?" Lexa quizzed as Dean finished writing

"Hard," Dean smiled as he looked up towards her. "Riley is most definitely a handful, but Daisy and I coping as best we can. I'm just grateful that she has a younger brother to babysit if needed." He replied as he stood back and straightened his uniform. "Is there anything else I can get you?" Lexa and Kim wave Dean's question politely away and he bowed slightly, turned and headed towards the kitchen.

"Before I forget, did Jacobson say any more about the extra shift you asked for?" Lexa asked, continuing their conversation.

"Yes, he did," Kimberley replied as she grabbed both of Lexa's hands. "Although it does mean that I'll be spending more time at the club." Lexa smiled and held Kimberley's hand tightly.

"Don't feel bad, you're able to spend more time doing what you love, just let me know if you need anyone, you know" Lexa punched the air just in front of her and resumed holding Kimberley's hand. She smiled at this and shook her head. More time had passed than either of them realised, as they were only pulled away from each other's gaze by Dean who had arrived next to their table. Their main courses in each of his hands. Lexa had ordered grilled salmon, crunchy new potatoes with a cream sauce and green beans. Kimberley, being a vegetarian, had ordered a simple noodle soup. They each smile at Dean as he placed their meals in front of them. Kimberley shook Dean's hand, stealthily passing him a tip, he smiled broadly at this and bowed away from their table again. Lexa picked up her fork and was about to start eating when her phone began to vibrate. Looking down, Lexa saw she had received a text.

"I thought the agreement was no phones at the table" Kimberley remarked reaching for it. Lexa grabbed the phone off the table before Kimberley could.

"That would normally be the case but after today I thought the rule could be relaxed slightly."

Kimberley smiled and nodded understandably. "Who's the message from?" she asked, picking up her chop sticks and starting on her meal.

"Dor, it seems he has to cancel our plans as... he is a witness to Olabode Taylor's trial... that's not what I expected." Lexa gave the message a quizzical look. The anger at Dorian's uncharacteristic resolution to Taylor's crimes relaxed slowly after hearing this news. All the things she knew about Dorian, his reaction to child slavery had put everything Lexa knew about him into question. Her brain turned wildly in trying to understand Dorian's thoughts.

"What do you mean sweetie, what has happened?" Kimberley questioned as she placed her cutlery next to her plate. "I thought Dorian had made arrangements, why has Mr Taylor been arrested?" Before Lexa could convey her own puzzlement, Dorian sends his explanation. As she read the message, her sceptical expression slid away. Lexa placed her phone into her trouser pocket. "He invoked the registration agreement. I don't know why I'm surprised, he is the champion of that disgrace of an 'agreement.'" The anger in Lexa's voice was calm, but Kimberley could tell how much this impacted her. She held Lexa's right hand in comfort, noting Lexa's other hand clenched into a fist on her lap. There was a small silence as Kimberley arranged her thoughts, Lexa's stern gaze shooting past Kimberley's shoulder.

"I know it's not easy, but maybe if it can be used to make the lives of those children better." Kimberley said tactfully, her stare kind and thoughtful. The registration Agreement had always been a difficult subject to talk about and was regularly avoided if it could be helped.

The agreement had come about thirty years ago, after several petitions to the world governments. At first, it had worked in settling people's worries, on all sides. It promoted fair and ethical treatment of the Drem. Giving them equal standing like they had never seen. In the following year after the registration, the newly formed registration police had gone from house to house; encouraging all powered people to register. With that came the great war between Steelhaven and their neighbour Verthollow.

Kimberley turned her hand so that her palm faced upward. "Do you mind if I have a look at the message, please?" she asked kindly, it took a while for Lexa to respond and only with a nod as she slid the phone over.

"I'm going to start eating" Lexa replied blankly. Kimberley pressed the touch ID button on the right side of the phone, finding the message and began to read.

      Hello Lexa, I hope you and Kimberley are doing well. I am afraid that I must change our plans for tonight. I didn't want to do it while you were there, if only to avoid things escalating further. I invoked Article six of the Registration Agreement. Hopefully, if all goes well the children will be in a better home by weeks' end. Also, considering I was unable to tell you the details of your suit delivery, it should be at your home at ten-fifteen tonight. It should meet all your expectations.

    See you soon, Dorian

"Do you know what Article six says? I can't quite remember" Kimberley asked softly.

"It's all about freedom from inhumane and degrading treatment." Lexa replied, not looking up from her plate. "It's something that he should have involved me in, without me, he wouldn't even know that it was going on. He's such a... never mind."

"That's an oddly specific time for a delivery, what do you think the reason is?" Kimberly asked, trying to ease out of the registration subject.

"I'm assuming it's because he wants to keep the amount of people who know to a minimum" Lexa replied, still not looking up. She stops abruptly, rests her own cutlery down on her half empty plate and sighs. "Sorry sweetie, I don't mean to snap." she whispered, getting an understanding smile back. "I just don't understand why he accepts that thing so readily when it's convenient, it promotes segregation on a global scale." Her voice trailed off as she looked back up through the skylight. Lexa's respect for Drem had not always been so strong, considering her own power only surfacing two years ago, Kimberley rested Lexa's phone down screen first and grabbed Lexa's forearm.

"I'm just glad no one knows about your ability." she whispered so that only Lexa could hear. "It keeps you in a better position to help people, especially know with the suit so you can keep your anonymity." Lexa nodded slowly in agreement. "Plus," Kimberly continued, "I'm sure you're going to look pretty damn fine in it." This got a loud laugh from Lexa which Kimberley echoed back.

The rest of their date continued without any more mention of Dorian or the situation. Focusing instead on the rest of their night. With Lexa visiting the Notpus hospital, where she works as a psychologist; with a speciality in psychoanalysis. Kimberly, on the other hand, would be going for her weekend shift at club Benzaiten's, where she works as the house singer. Their date concluded with a passionate kiss outside of the restaurant's entrance, drawing more attention than they wanted. Then they parted ways as their destinations were in opposite directions.

CHAPTER FOUR

As Kimberley waved goodbye to the last dozen or so of her fans that had kept her company between the restaurant and Aine's Attire, a franchised clothing shop that produces the finest dresses in all Steelhaven. She smiled to herself, grateful that she cannot just follow her dreams, but help her fans do the same in their own way.

"Welcome to Aine's Attire, how might I..." a well-dressed front of house began in automation as the bell rang when Kimberley walked through the shop's main entrance into the heart of the shop. A smile rose across his face. "Miss Sangster, it's just an honour to meet you, might I get you a glass of complimentary champagne for your shop today?"

"Yes, please...Julian." Kimberley replied as she read the greeter's name tag. "I'll start off browsing over in the main chamber, can you please let me know when my friends arrive?" Kimberley asked as they made their way down the main aisle. Julian agreed and bowed away to get her drink. Kimberley looked gleefully at the rows of mannequins lined on the back walls and on the raised platforms situated in a circle around the centre of a domed, white room. All dressed in high quality silk dresses in an assortment of colours and shades. When reaching the centre, she clasped her hands tightly to her chest and spun on the spot, her eyes closed in wonder. When she opened her eyes again, Kimberley was met by her first purchase. The peacock blue, silk dress on the mannequin shone brightly under the spotlight above. When Kimberley brushed her hand though the fabric, it melted along her hand like water. She closed her eyes again, imagining wearing it, with the beaded belt she had at home. Strolling down the aisle to the mannequin's right to two parallel rows of the same style of dress. She made a mental note of all the dresses she had an interest in. A slight breeze brushed past Kimberley's left shoulder, most likely from the skylight above. As she continued down to the end of the aisle, Kimberley noted another breeze on the same shoulder, harder than before. Turning around, she noted that it wasn't the wind but a teenage girl trying to get her attention. She stood not much shorter than Kimberley, her wavy black hair reaching her shoulders, hiding much of her face. There was a long streak of red next to her fringe. As her hand came back to rest with the other, the girl mumbled something quietly in her breathe.

"I'm very sorry, I was distracted, it's all so wonderful her. I hope everything alright." Kimberley stated, smiling reassuringly in hope to calm the girl's nerves.

"Hello, my name is Chloe Thesa, I'm your personal shopper today." The girl trembled, still full of nerves "...is, is there anything specifically you're looking for today?" Chloe's hands shook as she spoke, Kimberley could see the strain in trying to keep eye contact. The spot of red in her hair was being twisted in her right hand. Kimberley grabbed the lilac dress to her right, like the rest with a floral pattern made of beads.

"I was wondering if you could show me this dress in burgundy please." To Kimberley's surprise, instead of walking away to get the requested dress, Chloe reached out with her left hand and shifted the fabric between her fingers. A wave of colour spread across the dress until a dark shade of burgundy had enveloped it completely. Chloe looked down in worry. "You can control colour?" Kimberley wondered, looking Chloe up and down slightly.

"Chromakinesis, yes ma'am." Chloe whispered, her eyes still

looking at the floor. Kimberley smiled at this and looked back to examine the dress in more detail. Not only had the fabric colour changed but the beads had turned a bright shade of silver. They gleamed brightly as she turned the dress in the light. She was partly considering buying the dress, now that decision had been solidified.

"Ah I see you have already made your first choose," stated a voice from behind Kimberley. "A most splendid choice if I may say." Before Kimberley could turn around to face the source of the interruption, a figure had moved passed her and brushed Chloe aside. "Hello, my name is Isabelle Fuenta, I'm your personal shopper today. I can take that and get that wrapped up for you as you continue looking around." Isabelle stood high in her heels, the arch of the small of her back pushing her chest too high. The scarf around her neck kept her plated hair close to her shoulder. Her face plastered subtly with makeup, warm tones of brown and gold, making her green eyes and pearly white teeth stand out. "Might I recommend a low heel for that dress." Isabelle's voice was calm and warm, yet Kimberley could hear a trace of superiority. Kimberley looked behind Isabelle to see Chloe had begun to retreat back, her head further down. What Kimberley said made Chloe stop in her tracks and look up with wide eyes.

"I agree; however, I already have a personal shopper for today and I'm sure she is capable of showing me this, right Chloe?" Kimberley smiled at the surprise in both of their faces. Chloe nodded her head ever so slightly. She was unable to get past Isabelle. When Isabelle opened her mouth to respond, Kimberley thought of how Lexa would handle this situation and smiled.

"...and considering she had got here first" Kimberley continued proudly, reaching out a hand to which Chloe timidly took. "I don't see any reason to change now." The pair dashed away, giggling to themselves before Isabelle was too dumbstruck to speak.

"Thank you miss." Chloe whispered as they both slowed to a walk.

"Please, call me Kim and I only did the right thing, I know people generally don't like to have Drem assisting them but with yours. It'll help this shop go faster." Kimberley reassured the girl. Although she was happy to stand up for her, there was still a nagging worry creeping in. It wasn't because she was getting help from someone with power. She had never held a prejudice against them. Her friends on the other hand, weren't so open minded. This wasn't due to an active racial bias towards those with power, more of a cultural influence, a murmur in the back of the mind. So, when her friends arrived an hour later. She decided not to tell them of Chloe's ability. The news about Olabode Taylor and his shop was the only thing on their minds at any rate. As soon as Kimberley walked through the curtains separating the private fitting room to the rest of the shop, the large group rushed towards her with all manner of questions. Kimberley put her back to the curtain as they advance towards her.

"What did Sergeant Black do to the shop owner exactly? The news was so vague."

"What is he planning on doing with those children now under his control?" and

"I hear Alexandra was there with him, is that true?" Those were just a few of the questions thrown at her, each one overlapping the other. After a moment of this, Kimberley finally held her hands up, sat down and tried to answer all their questions. She also asked Chloe to use her ability outside of the room, for her own safety. She agreed, so when Kimberley wanted a new shade of dress, Chloe would stand outside for five to ten minutes then re-emerge with the 'new' dress. This tore at Kimberley, having to shamefully hide Chloe like that, but there was no other option, especially knowing two of her friends.

It took two hours before all the questions and gossip had been answered. This was mostly due to the small breaks for the main reason why they come to the place in the first place, dress shopping. Kimberley planned to premier several of her new songs at Benzaiten's that night, as well as record the performance on Holovinyl for sale to the general population. It's going to be a momentous day for her and if recent events hadn't happened it would be headline news. She wasn't affronted, she was glad in fact that those children were out of that situation. Well, maybe a little.

Kimberley and her friends had been so entranced by current situations that by the end of the shopping day, they had ordered over two dozen dresses. Whether Kimberley's friends knew about Chloe's abilities was debatable, the few that took an active interest in such things made no sign of their disgust. Kimberley had her first purchase, the burgundy dress from before, kept separate from the rest as she planned on wearing it that night. She and her friends chatted away as they passed the front counter, having already paid for their purchases in the fitting room. When she saw Chloe standing next to her fellow employees, she smiled at her. The smile was only partly returned, her eyes faint with a gaze that fell past Kimberley. The wave Kimberley sent after brought Chloe back to the present, a slither of warmth swept through her for a moment and she returns a small wave back, her hand low and out of sight.

"We hope to see you again." the rest of the employees announced in unison, Kimberley's smiled shifted up to the group as she left the shop.

Benzaiten's building used to be an old steel mill, one of the first of its kind to have its corrugated steel insulation heated with a special chemical solution sourced solely in Steelhaven itself. The only drawback to the first models was that they kept the walls ice cold to the touch, even in summer. So, when people lined up to enter the club, only those not local to the area rested on the building itself. An action they immediately regretted when the frost swam through them and shock down to the bone, which would last for hours. Thankfully, it was the last building of its kind to be housed in the centre of the city, as the rest had been demolished or modernized. As Kimberley past the club in her blue taxi, she noted a couple had already suffered this frost. Her concern didn't last long, as the bouncers of the club carried fur lined blankets over to them. The taxi stopped down at the end of the side alleyway, at the staff entrance. She stepped slowly out of the taxi, with help of the driver as she was wearing heels. She thanked him, passing over a twenty Konzar note as a tip. The driver thanked her as she passed through the back door into the club. Just after the steel mills moved out to the borders of Steelhaven, Benzaiten's was refurbished into a theatre, a feature still marked by the all the old posters of past plays all along when would have been the back-stage area. Most faded beyond recognition. Whenever Kimberley would walk passed them, she wondered what her life had been like, as an actress in those times. She would go back there, if only to hear Robert Cowell and Elena Solway in 'The greener grass.' A short, but powerful play about the last merchant royal family of Steelhaven and the binding love between the youngest son of the family and a Drem servant girl. Thinking back, Kimberley guessed that the play would not be so popular nowadays. Walking through the doorway at the end of the corridor. Kimberley was met by a sea of vanity mirrors for the other people that worked there, most being part of the band. Her back-up singer's tables were housed at the back of the room. Kimberley was grateful that no one was there so she could get ready without having to rehash the same story of the day again. It wasn't until she began her vocal warm ups did the others begin to arrive.

"Hey Kimmi, I hear that…" a voice to Kimberley's right began however, she glared over her shoulder, even if it was her best friend and lead back-up singer Sarah. There was a small silence between the two. "You're quite nervous about your performance tonight, I'm not surprised." Sarah continued as she walked over, sat down to the desk next to Kimberley and started applying her make up.

"I'm just worried that people won't like them, the new songs are different than what I normally sing." Kimberley replied in a quiet and sombre tone. Sarah looked over with concern and rest her hand on Kimberley's.

"It'll be fine, remember what our singing coach always says?"

"Confidence is always key." They recite in unison which seemed to relax Kimberley. She took a deep breath in and continued getting ready.

CHAPTER FIVE

It was five minutes passed ten and Lexa still was not home, although she was at least on the right street. Rechecking the time on her watch, she quickened her pace into a jog. Her loud strides echoing down the empty street. Both sides of the street lined with similar detached houses, their charcoal brick make them slightly indecipherable in the dark with only their small white porches and the glow of the street lights to illuminate them. It only took moments for Lexa to get from one end of the street to the other as she began to worry that she would be late to get home. She had left an hour later than she planned and now she had to rush. When she finally gets to her home, the panic in her heart fell away as she noticed there was no courier waiting at her front door. Walking up to the door and grabbed her keys out of her coat pocket, Lexa caught he breath and she sighed as her concern left her. As Lexa pushed the door open, the street light outside shining onto the stairs leading up to the rest of the house. The stairs are enclosed in walls of dark teal, the right wall ran up the stairs and was caped with a metal balcony. As she walked inside and flicked the switch to the right of the door. She pushed the door closed behind her with her foot. The light switch at the base of the stairs not only controlled the hanging light above her, but also the lights around the entrance to the living room. The bright light shown down, welcoming Lexa home. She hung up her coat inside the indent just right of the light switch, kicked off her shoes, and headed up the stairs.

The oak flooring of the stairs stretched across at the top, covering the entire floor, being stopped by the island separating her open-planned kitchen and the living room. In the centre of the room sat a set of chesterfields and a large wooden table matching the floor with the same dark shade of teal on the seats. Lexa brushed her fingertips on the back of the couch facing the large fireplace. Grabbing a bottle of water out of her fridge, Lexa walked over and placed it on the table as she passed it to start a fire to keep herself warm. Under normal circumstances, Lexa would look forward to watching the news upon returning home, recent events however, put her off it. Or watching any television for that matter and instead sat down with a book. The life and crimes of Walter T Arthur By Marcus Fletcher, this book told the story of a local serial killer, who was convinced that everyone he meet were Drem, including his parents. That psychosis pushed itself into a fear that would drive him to kill over two dozen people. All of them it turned out did not have powers after all. He was sentenced to firing squad for his crimes. This all happened four years ago. Several pages into the book, Lexa noticed blue flecks of light in the corner of her eye, after a third occurrence she stopped reading and looked up to the fireplace. Watching for a few moments with no more sightings, Lexa looked up towards the clock to the right of the fireplace. Half past ten Lexa calmly stood up and looked outside, no signs that anyone. She sat back down and check her phone, no missed calls. For some strange reason, one that she could not explain, Lexa stopped her investigation into finding her package and instead returned to watching the fire in search for the abnormal light. Moments after looking for said light, it emerged. The blue flame, brighter than she thought, its long body flickered and twisted around its fellows. The flame ventured in and out of view as it swam up and escaped into the chimney. Then a second and third appeared until all the seven-foot-tall fireplace shown bright with streams of blue flame. Lexa watched in awe as the heat reached out and covered her, she closed her eyes and smiled. When she opened them up, Lexa saw a small gap in the middle of the fire. Wanting to stand up and pass her hand through the newly formed gap, she tried to do so. Only to realise that she couldn't move a muscle, just sit and watch. Dread spread through her upon this realisation. She pushed against this unseen force to no avail, she was completely rooted to the spot. The hole in the fire widened until the fire had been divided clean in two. Lexa stared unblinking into the newly formed gap. Inside swam bright white stars, the constellations were like nothing she had seen before, Lexa's eyes began to tear up from the strain. Now when Lexa could take no more the unseen force vanished as fast as it had arrived, causing Lexa to fall forward. She slowly sat herself back up and saw that something had begun to push itself through the void. No, someone. The being pushed through completely until she stood confidently in front of the fire. Whoever it was, they stood clad head to heel in armour. The blue of the fire reflected brightly in the metal, making it hard for Lexa to see the person properly. The being stepped forward slowly, off the fireplace letting Lexa could see them fully. The blue in the double layered pauldrons and smooth helm faded back behind them. Lexa sat mesmerised without any thought of what to do. She hadn't even noticed that the chesterfield had moved from the left side of her to behind the mysterious figure. Not until the figure had moved their royal purple cape away to sat down.

"Ms Alexandra O'hearn?" the being's voiced echoed with the sound of several different voices speaking.

"Yes, that's me, who are you and what are you doing in my house?" she asked feeling as though she was pushing her luck already.

"It seems a mutual friend of ours has put an order in for some of our wares." The stranger continued as though they had not heard her response. "However, before we pass along anything, we require some questions to be answered." The stranger was sitting forward with their elbows on their knees, their fingers intertwined as they talked. Before Lexa could answer though, the stranger continued with their questions. "As the inquiry suggests, you will be using this suit to uphold your own personal morals. What makes your morals superior than others?"

"I'm going to use the suit to reinforce laws that already exist, whether my morals coincide with them or not." Lexa replied, feeling affronted by such an unneeded question or any line of questioning the suit is all payed for. Which she voiced to the stranger who again, did not respond for some time.

"You make it sound like we would want to be a part of yet another superhero adventure. As much as we respect Mr Black, his heroism did not end well. Now back to our questions, those laws that you are going to uphold, does that include the registration agreement? From what we hear are you not so accepting of it." The stranger retorts with calm indignation.

"The registration agreement is nothing but an unneeded law that is not..." the wall to Lexa's left suddenly implodes soundlessly, revealing not her bedroom but a dark alleyway with gunfire at the far end. Lexa turned her head in that direction only to be obstructed by a group of three soldiers that rushed past her right. The vanguard of the group rushing forward, blasting their assault rifle down the alleyway, the flashes on their gun spattering the backstreet with light. The second soldier rushed passed the first wielding a shotgun in both hands. The third stopped parallel to Lexa and blasted a long stream of electricity from both hands. As Lexa looked over at the soldier, she realised two things. Firstly, the whole situation was void of any sound and secondly, the electrokinetic's legs were phased through the coffee table in front of her. Lexa tried her hardest to remember all the critical information that she could. The electrokinetic had large copper coils protruding out of their backpack and one spiking out of each forearm, most likely there to increase the Drem's power. On his left pauldron was a trident branded, a symbol she would research afterwards. As they walked through the hole in Lexa's wall, a hurricane of bricks spreads around them, changing the scene to show the first two soldiers standing in front of a firing squad, their hands chained together and stapled to the floor.

"These men fought and died to protect your right for that freedom, they did this without thought for themselves or their morals." Gunfire blasted through the two prisoners, their heads held high right until the end. "They were true heroes." The frequency of the voice seems to sharpen as they said this and Lexa could hear a familiar voice in the sea of others, that of Dorian. "And the electrokinetic" they continued, "went through pain you could not imagine." The hurricane of bricks returned to change to a scene of the electrokinetic strapped to a laboratory slab, having his skin slowly peeled off by machines hovering above him. This scene only lasted a few seconds, but the screams lasted long past the rebuilding of the wall. They both snapped their eyes back to one another, "besides this isn't about laws, it's about justice, right?" The stranger questioned and now Lexa was certain that she had heard Dorian's voice, the situation seemed a lot more welcoming now. Seeing this less of an argument and more of a philological debate between friends.

"Under the right circumstances, they are one in the same with a few exceptions. If someone cheats in a relationship for example and the faithful partner decides to break everything the cheater owns, some would say that was justice." Lexa's voice had regained its strength and she sat back in her seat. She took a sip of the red wine in her hand, only to realise that she had any. She looked down at the glass with mistrust, placed the wine down and returned to staring at the stranger who had not moved an inch.

"Was it justice for Sternberg?" the calmness in the stranger's voice was not shared with Lexa's who sprang to her feet with such force that the couch behind her shoot against the wall, indenting it.

"Sirus Sternberg is a monster! He hurt more people than was ever publish reported in such horrific ways." Her voice on the last two words cracked as she felt herself close to tears, but her anger pushed her onwards. "So, don't you dare talk about things you know nothing about!" she screeched in frustration, which echoed around the room. The stranger remained unchanged by Lexa's outburst and let a silence hang between them for a while before responding. By the time they replied, Lexa had calmed down, yet still stood defiantly.

"When we saw the man, he was cutting words into his flesh and throwing food at the other patents in the mental institution he is now living in."

"What do you mean 'when you saw him?' What possible reason would you have to see that monster, or how for that matter?" Lexa questioned in puzzlement. Then she heard a scratching in the corner to the right of the fireplace, Lexa instantly knew what the cause was. Curled up in the corner, his long, matted hair obstructing much of his face. His left hand wrapped around his knees which were high against his chest. His right hand dragging against not the corner of her living room, but the concrete wall of Sternberg's cell. Before she could say anything, she heard an all too familiar sound. A low hum began to resonate all around the room, but it was unclear to find the source. Sternberg, however had begun a sharp, throaty laugh that shoot directed solely at Lexa. Their eyes pierced each other, resonating pure hate. A wide grin spread across Sternberg's face, a maddening smile which caused a periodical twitch in his head.

"Hey there cutie pie" Lexa's hands clasped fast around her mouth as a voice that was not hers sprang out. The humming around the room connected to Sternberg's laugh as it rang heavily, making the room shake. Lexa's hand moved sharply to her head, the pain began to grow harshly, she shut her mouth tight as she was too scared to open it again. The pain erupted and Lexa did the only thing she could. Lexa grasped out and began to crush the stranger's throat. She couldn't understand why they were doing this, they had been evaluating her past for no reason that she could understand. And if they knew all that Sternberg had done, then they should know all of what he had done to his victims. Whether they did not understand or did not care, then she would make them understand. Lexa pushed all the memories, all the pain onto the being who thought they could judge with their half truth.

Sternberg had hurt many people and gotten away with it. His first victim was a young man named Thomas Heatherton, only seventeen years old and living on the streets. He had been kicked out from his home six months before moving to Steelhaven. This was because of the power had been awoken inside of him, Cytokinesis. His parents were devastated and pushed him not only out of the house but out the border town where he had grown up. He would spend most of his days going from a food kitchen to his bed in the alleyway a few streets down. Sternberg was working there as a kitchen hand. He was very softly spoken and found it difficult to speak any other way. The two rarely saw each other, except for that one particular night. He was cleaning up after a day shift and Tom burst in, the diner had been closed for half an hour and empty apart from the two of them. Tom pleaded to get some food as he had arrived late, he had been across the other side of the city, going around all the local business, desperate to gain employment of any kind. It had been his third day without food and he wasn't taking no for an answer. Sternberg tried his best to explain that he wasn't physically able to gain access to the pantry as the manager had left with the keys. All he had was the front door key to lock up, but Tom refused to leave. His anger and hunger had gotten the best of him and in fit of rage, he threw several large spikes of ice at Sternberg, narrowly missing him as he was able to duck out of the way in time. That action triggered an anger inside Sternberg that he had never felt before. He grabbed a butcher's knife and, with his hatred flowing through him, he stabbed Tim repeatedly. Each thrust with more force than the last. As Tom's screams of pain died down so did Sternberg's red mist, allowing to see what he had done. He knelt over the body and frantically tried to stop the bleeding by pressing down hard with his hands. At that moment, a golden light began to pour out of them, he had no idea what was going on but was far too scared to move. The light filled Tim's body and burned so bright that Sternberg closed his eyes and lifted in his head as high as it could go. After a spell, he slowly lowered his gaze back down, terrified as what had just happened. To his amazement however, Tim was not dying in front of him, but quietly gasping for breath. The deep cuts that Sternberg would see were closing up by themselves. He jumped up and backed away, no matter what had caused this, Sternberg knew that he could not stay there. He rushed out into the street and ran, ran so far that he collapsed over five miles away, out of cheer exhaustion.

It was there when Sternberg met his second victim, Michael Frost, another Drem. When Michael discovered Sternberg's collapsed body laying in the middle of the road, he tried to steal his wallet. Michael had lived on the street for over five years before that moment and he was desperate. As soon as Michael grabbed for Sternberg's brown coat however he woke up and began to beat the young man out of sheer panic. Blood flowed in the air and marked the snow around them. When he had finished, Michael's face was completely collapsed in on itself. Unlike a few hours before, Sternberg didn't panic and instead reached out again, knowing he could command this power. Golden light flushed through his hands and when the light licked over Michael's flesh, it slowly reconstructed, allowing Michael to breath with ease again. A call of laughter echoed around the empty road the pair. With a broad smile, he repeated his attack. This continued, making the healing rate faster with every repetition, until he could no longer lift his arms. He then picked himself off the ground and began walk off down the street, whistling a small tune to myself.

His third and fourth victims were a couple out on a date, Gavin Jackson and Heather Marshall. Gavin worked at a steel mill, coating corrugated steel with a solution that when heated to a high enough temperature would increase the strength of the

metal ten fold. Heather went to the local university, studying to be an architect. They were walking home after a romantic meal at their favourite restaurant, when Sternberg attacked them from behind with a metal baseball bat. First Gavin and then Heather before she could realise what had happened. Sternberg had taken a month and all his savings to prepare an efficient kill room. He had brought a small warehouse, not much bigger than a few square feet, on the northern border of Steelhaven. It had originally been a quarry site for the naturally occurring steel mined from the cliff side. That was many years ago. Sternberg put down large sheets of plastic and covered himself in the same to protect himself from the splatter of blood.
He tied them facing each and then proceeded to torture the one while the other sat helpless.

Golden spiritual copies of each of the victims began to spawn around Lexa, each standing strong with her, defiant. Before she knew what hit her however, Lexa was flung onto her back. She opened her eyes to see the being had lost its helm to reveal a teenage girl. Her face like stone, short royal purple hair on one side and shaved on the other. When Lexa stood back up, the being walked forward making Lexa retreat. As the armoured girl spoke streams of tears fell across her cheeks. These tears boiled half way down her cheeks and evaporate.

"The others expected that you would react this way, although I protested your integrity." A high-pitched screech sprang out from the fire. Lexa looked behind the girl, she watched as creatures made of the celestial darkness began to flow out of the void, the unknown constellations melting into them. They flooded into the room, crawling over one another, encircling the pair. "I thought your training to be our protector would calm your judgement, but alas your pride continues to be prominent." Lexa had to keep the creatures at arm's length as they try to push against her, but she couldn't. The creatures continued to pour in from the fireplace until it was difficult to move. "So, I am afraid that our wares are no longer available for your purchase." The

gentle brushing of the creatures turned to a full blown attack as they begun to claw and bite at Lexa, dragging her down. She screamed and struggled against them but there was no use. She couldn't move as they slowly closed off her airway.
There was nothing she could do.

Lexa woke up in a panic, gasping wildly for breath and stretching out in desperation. The mist in her eyes cleared as she regained focus to see her living room again. Looking up on instinct to the clock, it was exactly ten-fifteen. Perhaps she had dozed off but woke up just in time for the courier to arrive, but then she looked down at the coffee table in front of her. The same briefcase full of money that Lexa had originally giving Dorian to pay for her suit. On top of the case was stapled a note titled 'Rejection'. Reading through the note, her heart sank as she sat back to stared at the fire once more.

CHAPTER SIX

It had been four years since Malik had been inside the registration building, the first time was when his father had dragged him in to register and get freed on the same day. Being both his employer and his father, he was within his right to do so. This time he was in line to register for a power tracker, Malik felt nothing but fear. The power tracker recorded any usage of the individuals power wearing it. The apparatus was required by law by all registered Drem that interact with the public as a profession. While he was no longer lawfully required to wear one, he felt a strong obligation for one, now that he was the new owner of his father's business. This was because, after the trial, where his father had been given a ten-year sentence. Malik had been passed ownership of the Smith and Taylor; much to Olabode's furious objection. The first week in business however, did not go well as there had been zero customers since the shop's grand reopening. This was disgraceful in his eyes, considering the number of customers he saw had guns strapped to their hips while they were shopping. He voiced this opinion to a few of the queue around him. After the first hour, they choose to turn deaf ear, so Malik looked around for another distraction. The building looked hundreds of years old, it's stone walls shoot high above him, holding each ascending floor around its edges. The centre of each floor had been cut out, to allow a strong beam of sunlight to shot through the skylight in the roof. Malik stared up in wonder at the clouds floating by.

"Next!" a voice came from in front of him which he ignored. Only after several louder repeating of that demand, did Malik respond. Malik saw a middle-aged man sitting behind the counter. His weathered face and the vacant look in his eyes made Malik feel quite intimidated. He curled his hand to beacon Malik forward. Before he could say anything, the man had ripped the paper out his hand, stamped it and told Malik to move over to another queue, before shouted for the customer behind to move forward. Given the fact Malik had been for over three hours already for the newly stamped form only for it to tell him that he needs to join another line and start the process all over again. Malik decided to take a break and instead of joining the new queue straight away, he went across to the canteen and ordered three different types of chocolate, one with nuts, a packet of salt and vinegar crisps and an fruit drink. Searching for a place to sit, Malik noticed someone he never thought he would see again, let alone in this building. Lexa. Her long auburn hair covered much of her face, but Malik had no trouble recognising her.

"Hey. What are you doing here? I didn't think this was your kind of place." He asked, walking over and placing his tray opposite hers. After a moment of silence however, Malik continued. "Well hopefully you're doing better, I've been here since the place opened and only been to two people so far." Malik broke off a large block of chocolate and crams it down. "...all I want is a power tracker so I can get the business back to the way it was, that shouldn't be that hard, right?" Lexa didn't move, not even to eat the bowl of soup in front of her. She just stared out, Malik wasn't sure she had noticed he was there. He sighed to himself and focused on his lunch instead. Malik grabbed the last of his sandwich and spun around in his seat to find the queue he needed. The lines of deadened faces caused a sadness in his heart, Malik tried to stay optimistic and explained the sadness away with the bitter chill. This wasn't because of the outside as it was quite a warm day. In fact, he had been given advice from those who had visited the registration building, to bring warm clothes. He was glad he had as those who didn't, left the building within the hour. As Malik gaze panned across the snakes of lines around him, he noticed a small group of children. They couldn't be much younger than he was. They stood enveloped in thick, fur lined clothing with only a small gap between their hats and scarves to see through. The pair of children closest to the rope separating the lines looked up and down, noting the coast was clear. Turning back, they nod eagerly to the tallest of the three, who nodded back. They pull down their scarf and took off their gloves. Malik was puzzled by this, especially as the tallest child scooped their hands together to their mouths to blow warm breath on them. Malik turned fully around to watch. The child breathed deep into their hands and then rub them together, after several times of this happening, flickers of flames flew out of the gaps in their clasped hands. The other two moved closer, their hands outstretched. After a final and hard breath, the leader opened their hands and a sharp burst of flame erupted high in the air. Thankfully not too high for the flames to be seen above those around them. They smile, watching the warmth sweep through several people around them. Their fleeting spurt of hope was dashed away by someone passing outside the regulated lines. A military police officer, he grabbed the lead child's hands, shutting them closed and extinguishing the fire, dragging the child away. There was no objection from anyone within view, not even from the child's friends who had dropped their heads instantly, pushing their hands around their sides in hopes to keep a hold of some of the heat. Malik smiled at this, served them right for not following the rules he thought to himself. He voiced this to Lexa, a little too loud, she still gave no response.

"Because there are rules, regardless how innocent it may be, it could have quickly become too dangerous. For example," Malik projected the last few words as Lexa had finally looked over at him. "Say that guy behind those kids had become startled, thinking there were a fire. He could have stumbled back and knocked the kid over, which would have fanned that flame over dozen in front of them." That's a little extreme Malik thought, but it was valid. Lexa smiled softly.

"It's never that simple; at least that's what Dorian always says"

"Well that's patronizing." Malik blurts out which made Lexa laugh and nod her head.

It was over an hour before they had realised that they had forgotten why they were there and focused only on their discussion on all that happened at the trial of Malik's father and the aftermath. The lines had doubled since they started and when Malik realised this, he stood up and took his rubbish over to a nearby bin. When he returned to the table, Lexa was on the phone, as he sat down, he noticed how tense she had become. While she was busy on the phone, Malik went back to watching those around him. To the young group of men watching the news on the large screen above the entrance. To the elderly gentlemen helping his wife stay warm with a quilted blanket. When his gaze had landed on the cashier of the canteen, he overheard what Lexa was saying and felt a powerful urge to listen.

"7.22, 9.53, 11.35. What do you have?" Maybe she was planning on coming back for a meal here. However, on checking the large printed menu over the counter, none of those prices were there. "I'm not sure if I'm ready for this, are you sure you can't…" she was cut off by the person on the phone, which made her shift slightly in her chair. "No, no I understand. I'll see you when this is over." Ending the call and placing her phone back in her pocket, she rubbed her eyes with her right hand.

"Are you alright? I hope it wasn't more bad news." Malik questioned, trying not to push her too much as she was clearly worried about something important. When she dropped her hand, focused back on Malik, her eyes widen in surprise as though she had just remembered he was there.

"Kid, I need you to do something for me and you can't ask

why or grab too much attention." The sternness in her voice made it hard for Malik to ask anything, something serious was happening and it shot fear right through him. "I need you to make a distraction over there." She continued, pointing towards the central holdings where all the lines ended. The collection of counters stood ten-foot-tall and made of blackened oak, each carved with the registration symbol under each employee.

"I can try, but I'm not sure how effective I can be." Malik replied with concern. Lexa nodded back understandably and looked around. After a sweeping look across the crowd, Lexa pointed over the group of children from before. Malik instantly knew what Lexa had planned. He rejected this idea with a shake of his head.

"It's okay, it's okay, just keep safe" she sighed quietly as she stood up, turning on the spot and striding over to a small group closest to them. The pair of men were standing next to the wooden separator of the canteen entrance. They were drinking from cardboard cups and talking amongst themselves. There was nothing overly strange about them, it wasn't until one lifted his drink up for another swig did Malik notice the Omegan symbol tattooed on the man's inner wrist. Panicked, he watched as Lexa strode powerfully towards them. He stood up stiffly, trying not to draw any attention to himself and walked calmly towards the canteen counter, to get somewhere safe as soon as possible. Part way there, he heard the gunfire and screams. He dove forward to gain cover around the bin on the corner of the canteen before the masses of the people rushed past him. When he finally caught his breath, Malik peeked over the bin to watch the fight and move if got to close to him. Lexa had already dispatched the pair she had begun with and had vanished out of sight. What were Omegan fighters doing here of all places? Another pair, a man and woman ran passed him, holding guns high and ready to fire. He wasn't sure why he did it, maybe to protect Lexa or maybe just a gut reaction of self-preservation. Whatever the reason was, his actions had dire consequences. As soon as he heard one of them scream out Lexa's newly discovered location Malik stood up and reached out and twisted their emotions so quickly and in numerous directions that the pair collapsed to the floor and dropping their weapons. Malik stood paralysed with fear, what had he done? Looking over he saw Lexa, she was panting with her long hair sprayed wildly. She smiled strongly over at him and gave him a small nod. Before he could try and respond however, a sudden and powerful blow to Malik's head slammed him into the ground. Dazed, Malik slowly looked around, blood pouring out of a cut above his right eye. His attacker's blooded shadow pulled their rifle back for another attack. While blurred shadows of more soldiers rushing forward behind him to attack Lexa. Malik shook madly, trying to wipe the blood from his eyes, terrified that this would be the last thing he would ever see. Holding his other arm high in a desperate attempt to protect himself. His mouth quivering to find something, anything to say that would save his life, but nothing came to mind. Whatever attack was launched at him was cancelled out by the buildings defensive shutters crashing to the ground at the front gate. The four-ton block of concrete that melded out of the wall above, hit the ground with such force that it created a cloud of dust that spread across much of the ground level. He knew this would not save him however, Malik slowly lowered his arms and tried his utmost to steady his breath, he would face his death with the small amount of dignity he had left. A hand gripped his forearm and dragged him to his feet.

"Stay calm little one, you need to move quickly." A familiar voice calmly spoke to him, as he wiped clean his eyes, he saw through the patched smoke that it wasn't his attacker commanding him, but Lexa. Her eyes shone brightly through the dust cloud and she moved Malik across to the rest of the group she had collected and together they walked across the hall. They travelled tightly together, some holding hands to stay close. The smoke had began to clear and to the groups horror there stood over a dozen figures, each holding assault rifles. They stopped and dropped to their knees and pleaded for mercy. Lexa continued walking, turned around when she realised no one else had continued. She beckoned them to follow. None of them moved, far too paralysed with fear. To Malik's terror, Lexa spoke to one of the attackers, he stroked his wavy beard as he replied and signalled the rest to move forward. On instinct Malik stood up high and prepared himself to attack. It was Lexa that stopped him with a shake of her head. He stared back bemused, he had no intention on dying today but something stopped him from defending himself. For some strange reason, he trusted Lexa's intentions and waited. As the hostile group continued forward however, this trust lessened, and he began to move forward again. Instead of attacking them however, the hostile pack walked passed their hostages before he could move far. One of them brushed Malik's shoulder as they continued walking. Malik watched them as they headed towards the flight of stairs leading to the second floor, seemingly oblivious to anyone in front of them. When they were out of view, Malik turned back to Lexa, who again beckoned them to follow her. None of the hostages hesitated this time and followed her to the side exit of the building, to safety.

Being a man of little patients, Dorian took little interest in the police officers' cheers and attempts to talk to him as he walked down the prison corridor toward prisoner holdings. Even to go as far as lifting some aside so he could get passed. This angered several of them and they voiced their discomfort loudly. Getting to the end of the hallway, Dorian pulled open the door and strode in to find an elderly woman sitting at a desk. She had curly white hair, some of which was pulled back into a bun, most was draped down to her shoulders. She wore thick round glasses which amplified the size of her eyes. As he walked in, she looked up from her computer, her gaze already forgetting his presence. "Yes? can I help you young man?" Her raspy voice echoed around the room. As she said this, she moved across to the other side of her desk to glance down at a clip board.

"Yes ma'am, I am here to vouch for Ms Alexandra O'hearn, I hear she is being kept on relaxed charges of public endangerment." They both outstretched their arms when Dorian had reached the desk and shook hands firmly. "I hope she is not giving you too much trouble." He finished, hoping this was indeed the case. The woman did not respond to this but instead looked down her list. Halfway down, she noted Lexa's information.

"How do you know the accused?" She asked coldly, resting her right index finger just below the found information as she looked back up.

"She's my therapist." Dorian replied, passing over documentation confirming that. As she took the papers off him, Dorian spoke them aloud. This was for the record of the cameras that were housed in every corner of the room.

"One email conformation from Steelhaven hospital, listing the client, the doctor and the relevant time of said appointment.
Three printed photographs of personal outings involving the accused and her guarantor.
Six hand written letters illustrating the extent of the relationship between the accused and her guarantor.
 One explaining the reasoning behind the accused being at the registration building that day.
I hope that will be satisfactory." Dorian concluded. On inspecting the documentation, the clerk agreed and lead Dorian through the door behind her to the holding pen beyond.

The room stretched further than the eye could see, light only by the hanging lights above. On either side of the room were three raised platforms protruding upward in ascending order towards the inner walls. Those platforms held the prisoners who; instead of being locked in cages, where chained to the ground. They sat in a kneeling position, the chains held their arms behind their backs and head facing the ground. It was relatively easy to monitor them from the raised cross walks at regular intervals across the breadth of the room. The clerk shuffled to the console directly in front of her and pressed in the number allocated to Lexa. "I hope she has been treated fairly at least." Dorian questioned as he watched the large crane on the ceiling move smoothly and quietly to where Lexa was being held far down the room.

"No more than the rest, I can assure you." The clerk crooked back.

"Even after the charges were dropped?" Dorian asked with more force, stepping forward to meet the prisoner block holding Lexa.

"That's not how it works here, now remember, she only has three days left to find an appropriate job before she gets drafted into the military." The clerk concluded and handed Dorian papers to sign. The prisoner block falls into the designated space for prisoner transfer, the chains holding Lexa down dropped to the floor and slide back into their clamps. Dorian reached out his hand which Lexa gladly, if slightly weakly accepted.

It wasn't until Lexa had bathed, rested, and eaten before Dorian even attempted to her to explain what had happened in her own words. Perhaps she had not been ready for her first solo outing. Even if she had been Dorian thought, the actual attempt of such things can go wrong far too easily. Dorian knew this all too well about that. When they finally did talk about the situation, Lexa's words were chosen very carefully and whispered to begin with, before she could find her strength again. Lexa used her power to change the memories of the attackers in real time, she disguised herself as one of them and made them think the hostages had ran to the second floor in the confusion of Lexa's initial attack.

"What job are you thinking about? I can remember in your letter that you were thinking about law enforcement, Is that still the case?" Dorian passed over a mug of black coffee as he asked. Lexa took a large gulp and smiled.

"I know, today didn't help but yes, it's the best position to go into. And before you say anything, no, this is not because of the rejection from the others, it was ultimately their choose on whether I deserved the armour or not." Lexa explained as Dorian pulled ingredients from the cabinets in Lexa's kitchen to make himself a sandwich.

"Are you certain of that? The whole reason why you were there in the first place was because of that night."

"Yes, I am sure. In fact, when I was hold up at the police station. I thought to myself that maybe they saw this happening." Dorian just shot her an unconvinced look. "Think about it, I'm guessing their ability to project into dreams, that perhaps they also possess some sort of foresight. Many predictions about the future have been through precognitive dreaming."

"Not in the way you think." Dorian replied as he finished his lunch. "Precognition is an unreliable ability at the best of times. Because knowing of a potential future change it instantly."

"Unless that information was already predetermined to be known at that time." Lexa countered, she always did enjoy debating such matters.

This discussion continued for several hours and was only disrupted by someone coming through the front door.

"Alexandra, are you home?" a concerned voice shouted up.

"Yes, I'm here. I'm glad you got my text…" Lexa began, but is cut off by Kimberley as she had walked up the stairs, without saying a word and pulled Lexa into a fierce embrace. "I'm just glad I was able to help. It was worrying at first, I just went on instinct for the most part." She continued, wrapping her arms around her girlfriend.

"…and it's good that she did, otherwise who knows what could have happened." Dorian interrupted, but was meet not with gratitude as he thought, but a sharp slap across the face. This shocked even Lexa who stepped forward to apologise, but Kimberley held up her hand to stop her.

"Don't you talk to me about what was good, she could have died, and you were nowhere to be seen!" Her hand rose for another hit, but Dorian pushed it back with his power.

"Don't push it." he finished, creating a short silence that was only broken when Lexa told Kimberley her career chooses.

"Because you didn't get enough of their cruel treatment today?" was Kimberley's first response to which Lexa chuckled.

"That's why I must join, to try and change the treatment for our kind." Lexa gestured to both herself and Dorian to emphasize her point. "I'm not saying that everything will change overnight, but I can't just sit back and do nothing, and I know you'd get tired of me complaining eventually." That got a smile out of Kimberley. Lexa pulled her close, "I need you to take over my duties at the support group permanently, if that's alright." Kimberley sighed through her smile but she eventually agreed. "Don't worry I'll be safe, I haven't even applied yet. I'm sure I'll get in though, right Dor?" Lexa turned to ask Dorian only to notice he had left without saying a word. "I hate when he does that."

CHAPTER SEVEN

Two weeks after the attack on the registration building, the cleaners Malik had hired were still removing the offensive, racial slurs of graffiti plastered over his newly opened shop. 'Defilers', 'cursed ones' and 'abominations' were just a few of them. Walking through the restored showroom of his shop to what used to be his father's office, he felt thankful that his father's estate could cover the damages.

As he sat down behind the dark oak writing desk, he remembered the first sight he saw after returning to open the shop. The whole building had been set alight, filling the air with mounds of smoke. Walking into the shop's office to find it had been untouched. Not just that, but nothing was out of place. The family photos housed beyond the desk, the dozens of pristine books that Malik could never touch. Even the carpet made from the finest silk were all still there. Sitting at the desk Malik's confused dissolved away when he saw a hand-written letter laying against the wooden fountain pen holder.

>To the child reckless who used his power against us,
>We the Omegans, who are tasked to defend humanity against you cursed ones.
>You selfish beings who thought they could steal from the gods and become divine yourself.
>We, the guardians of those who can't defend themselves.
>We judge you Malik Taylor as our enemy.

We will do all within our power to destroy you and those just like you.

Consider this a warning.

Thankfully, there was no second warning waiting for him since then
Malik stretched wildly and began to organise the workers for the third re-opening. Most of the children that worked under his father, choose to stay and continue working in the shop. Just after the trail in fact, they all sat down and worked out a contract for the workers to keep them safe. Which included the redecoration of their rooms down in the basement. That was handled mostly by the courts as it was a part of Malik's own agreement with them to have better accommodation. Malik kept that from them however, he wanted it to appear as though it was his idea and they were very grateful. Over the next month, the shop and its basement would be completely refurbished. The wooden displays had been replaced with marble mannequins on raised platforms. Malik had also entered an advertisement in the local newspaper for apprising artists to get in contact in display their work in his shop free of charge. Malik got regular artist's bringing their work in every week. Everything seemed to be going well until Malik received his first visitor.

He was a tall, thin man with a receding hairline gelled back in place. He was welcomed but walked past the counter and into Malik's office. Malik stood up to greet the man but was ignored.
"Mr Bashert." He proclaimed as he walked past Malik and sat behind at his desk, resting his boney hands on his briefcase. He reached into his vest coat pocket to pull out a silver pocket watch. He stared at the watch for a moment and placed it back. He icy glare through Malik off. Tired of waiting for a response, Mr Bashert sighed heavily.
"Excuse me, can I help you with something?" Malik questioned as the man sat behind the office desk and placed a worn, leather briefcase in front of him. He pulled out a folder and began to read

through it. "I don't know what's happening, but this is my office. All our suits here are custom made to fit the customers' needs. If you're looking for anything in particular..." Malik asked with restraint, still having the power tracker strapped firmly around his right upper arm and no way to take it off without the law finding out, at least not until closing time. That was over four hours away, it showed on his face, Mr Bashert's thin lips curled into a smile.

"I'm here at the request of your father, to oversee his investments. Here is the newly forged agreement that I need you to sign so we can continue." He past the folder over and Malik read it through. It confirms all he said, the ownership would transfer to Mr Bashert to keep hold of, until his father's sentence was complete. At that time, the ownership of the shop, the house behind the shop and several other investments would once again be back under his father's control. As Malik read the letter, he slowly sat down in one of the chairs facing the desk. The blood in his face slowly drained and when he was done, Malik closed his eyes, took a deep breath in and said the only thing he could think of.

"I would need my own lawyer to go over this before we continue, I'm afraid." Malik's hands rested calmly on his lap, trying not to show his sorrow that his father would go down this road. Malik's brain ran in cycles trying to find someone who could help him. All while Mr Bashert collected his papers back up, calming exclaiming that Malik was making this transition difficult and that he would be back at the end of the month to conclude the transfer. His booming instructions falling on deaf ears as Malik simply stared ahead at a group of photos resting on the shelf behind his desk. One of his father shaking hand with the major, a broad smile stretched across his face and the other, his father standing in front of the shop with pride. The last picture was overshadowed by the other two so much that it could barely be seen. It was that of the only photo Malik had of them together on the happiest day of his life. He had taken it on his eight birthday with the Polaroid camera that had been his fathers, when he was around that age. Malik had found it while was playing hide and seek, hiding in his father's wardrobe. It was stuffed in a box with some other items from his father's past. A book on herbalism, old photographs of Malik's grandparents and a pocket telescope. Malik used one of his father's belt to chain the doors of the wardrobes closed. He felt so close to his father at that moment, having heard nothing about his childhood or even what his parents were like; as his father rarely spoke to him. Three hours past and his seekers hadn't found him. Later Malik would find out it was because they had gone out to play football in the garden instead. They weren't his friends, but children of his father's friends, he took no notice of this as the treasure he had found was more important. Plucking up enough courage, Malik grabbed the camera and rushed down show his father what he had found.

Olabode Taylor was sitting at the fireplace talking to a person Malik had never seen before with his back to the door. Malik rushed the pair and grabbed his father's right arm in a tight embrace. To Malik's surprise his father laughed joyously at this, picked his son up and sat him on his lap. The glazed look Malik normally got from his father was replaced with a shine that filled his face.

"Well, hello there birthday boy. What do you have there in your hand son?" Olabode grabbed the camera out of Malik's hands. "I haven't seen this in nearly thirty years, where did you find this?" He nodded at the gentleman he was talking as he saw the man got up to leave. Undeterred by his father's sudden attitude change towards him, or choosing to ignore the obvious, Malik grabbed the camera back. He stood on his father's lap and with an outstretched arm, snapped a picture of the two. They sat there talking about all the questions Malik ever wanted answers to, stopping only to cut the cake, play some games with the other children and see the guests off. Deep down Malik knew he was driving the emotional outburst of affection from his father.

Malik's pure joy at finally connecting with the man that gave him life, had bonded with his power at that moment and pulled those feeling out. The consequences would come later, and they always did, in spades. The treatment Malik received from his father was more bearable after that. It was never right however, and he did all he could to protect himself and the other children working in the shop. But now that he had seen that side of his father, the kind man he could be. Malik covertly repeated the same thing for days as he could within the month without his father noticing. This had spared the others from his father's wraith he said to himself and he begged it to be true. The room was empty when Malik focused back to his surroundings and knew what he had to do.

The prison was housed far in the outskirts of the city, enclosed in the forest at the base of mount Ashford to the north. The mountain stood so high above that it held the sun away from the prison, leaving it in shadow for most the day. It was not difficult for Malik to see his father, given that he had sent his lawyer over, Olabode had been expecting him. He knew his son too well.

"What are you doing father? The courts gave me full control over the family estate." Were the first words Olabode heard and he laughed at them, cutting his son off mid-sentence. Why shouldn't he protect his inheritance from his kind? He thought to himself. Son or no, Smith and Taylor had been in his family for near two hundred years, ever since his great, great, great grandfather stole it from under his business partner Solas Smith. And he wasn't about to let a Drem control something he had not right to. Olabode sat high in his chair, lording over his son. Malik lowered his head on instinct. Olabode surveyed his son and found him wanting, the inferior way he held himself, hunched shoulders and averting his gaze, spoke volumes. His son could not be trusted with his legacy. An upstart such as him would run the business into the ground. He said none of this however and choose instead to keep a stare on his son. "I've been running it for over a month and the profits have been steadily raising back to where they used to be, I don't understand what changed in that..." Olabode raised his right palm up for his son to be silent and so he did, without question. Placing his hand back down, Olabode returned to staring him down and saying nothing. After twenty minutes of silence, the visit was over, and the guard came to escort Malik out.

Just as he was leaving Malik turned back to look at his father. "I'm sorry."

CHAPTER EIGHT

"You shouldn't take it heart sweetie." Kimberley tried to reassure Lexa as they walked back into their home for the night. She could see all the change in attitude towards her was taking its toll. As she followed her up the stairs, Kimberley noticed Lexa shaking.

"It's difficult not to, the way they looked at us at the restaurant was disrespectful. Nothing has changed, people are just found out a different side of me." She walked over and sat on the chesterfield with Kimberley following suit, sitting on her lap. Lexa began to cry silently, her cold face stuck on how to react. Kimberley wipes Lexa's left cheek, kissing it and wraps her arms around her.

"They just have to get used to it sweetie, it'll just take time." Kimberley held Lexa tightly for a moment and stood up. "On a more pleasant subject, I have a surprise for you." Walking into their bedroom, Kimberley reached into the top draw of her bedside cabinet and pulled out a small box. "Before you get too excited, it's not a ring." She jokes, seeing the shocked look on Lexa's face. Lexa slowly opened the box and bounced with glee when she saw what was inside. An onyx medallion shaped in a three-headed falcon hung on a beaded necklace, at the clasp was a metal band inscribed with the words. 'Change brings strength.' The necklace had once belonged to her father. It had been a reassuring gift from him after they moved to Steelhaven, to remind herself that change wasn't always bad. She lost the necklace in the incident that woke her power.

"Where did you find it? I've been looking for it for years." Lexa asked, pulling on the small necklace.

"That's a secret," Kimberley replied with a smile. "I've kept it for a while, for the right moment. When you really needed it. Remember sweetie, I'll always be here to support you throughout everything." Kimberley saddles Lexa's lap again and kisses her fiercely. Running her hand through her hair, twisting the ends in her fingers.

They sat like this for a while, just enjoying each other's company, then Lexa turned to her girlfriend.

"How did the record executives take the idea about selling your Holovinyl in Verthollow?"

"They were very open to it, in fact before they send me on tour. They are thinking about putting me on a spike projector." Lexa sits up and rests her hands-on Kimberley's thighs. Lexa wasn't so sure about that technology, mostly because she hasn't had little experience with them. A spike projector used sonic vibrations and magnetism to project long and thin spikes to form any shape required. Spike projectors were mostly used for educational or official purposes.

"That's fantastic, congratulations. When does it start?"

"Pretty much after the Holovinyl is released over there, they want me more active in promoting my music. They even gave me some of the posters they're putting up around town." And they sat looking at the holographic posters that promoted Kimberley's next album. Rivers of light. Kimberley treasured every moment of that night, knowing that in the morning would mean that Lexa would be moving out and starting her new career.

The graduation parade was held at noon, the sun shone high over the marble walls of the police academy, the stage for the ceremony stood in front of the main entrance. It towered over the crowd, eclipsing the first few rows of the graduates. The orchestra, that was adjacent to either side of the stage began to play loudly and silenced the muttering crowd as Christof Macbay, Police Chief to all of Steelhaven, stepped on stage. Around sixty years old, Lexa was sure that he was one of the few that had lived much of his twenties before the registration event. He swaggered up the stairs to the podium in his official uniform. His right shoulder plastered in medals. His confidence beaming across the crowd, a broad grin across his face as he began his speech.

"Ladies and gentlemen of Steelhaven," His booming voice made an echo through the pa system. "It's a great honour to be presenting this graduate class to you, the people they will be protecting. I can remember my own ceremony a few years ago." A laugh broke out in the audience above the graduates which Macbay casually waved aside. "My father, Charles, had stood in this very spot and handed me my diploma. I'm proud to follow that tradition my son." Lexa looked across to the person several rows in front of her, Dean, who smiled and shook his head. Dean had been one of the few friends Lexa had earned with basic training. With her Drem ability, and training with Dorian, Lexa had flown through the required training in a month. Whereas the rest had spent over two years studying the law. This caused a strong resentment to build between her and the rest of the cadets. Even the other Drem avoided her. This isolation might also have had something to do with the article Lexa posted on the academy forum, it presented historical evidence of how powered people had evolved alongside Humankind and that social/religious conventions pushed the groups apart. Only for Humankind to use those same passages from their holy book to subjugate the Drem. All the cadets shunned her, all except Dean, who instead of vilifying her, routinely visited her with such accuracy that she would have a mug of coffee ready when he arrived. This friendship also helped him get Summa Cum Laude in his class, even above Lexa herself. Although Dean's father may have had a hand in that also. As Captain Macbay continued with his speech, Lexa looked down at her new badge, A kite shield, red with gold spear and Copper flintlock crossed behind. She was finally a part of something bigger than herself. Brimming with pride she polished it with her thumb. The sun pierced through the gap in the roof of the station and gleamed over the badge that sat high on her chest. Next to the badge Lexa held a ceremonial rifle. Comprised of mostly brass, the flintlock rifle had a giant scope housed on top. It had originally been the official weapon for the police over a century ago. It was seldom used now however, for its sheer size made it impractical for the modern age. A loud trumpet brought Lexa back to the present and the other cadets had stood up began to line up to walk in single file to the podium. Although there was no segregation in the graduate lines, when they received their diploma there were two people standing parallel to Captain Macbay. The person to his right had a white scorpion patched in a circle on their chest. The ancient symbol of the Drem'onor. The person on the opposite side had the symbol of the rest of humanity, a golden hand. All three of them stood with a smile wide on their faces and arms outstretched. Without thinking the graduates split into two as they reached the trio. It took over two hours to complete the hand over and at the end, the cadets stood behind the captain, facing the crowd as it cheered in celebration. In moving from her position in the ceremony to the podium, Lexa had lost where Kimberley was sitting. But it didn't take her long to find her, she outstretched her right arm overhead and cheered loudly, projecting her happiness over to her. In recognition of Lexa and the crowd turning to look at her, Kimberley sent a small wave back, feeling embarrassed. Lexa however, was not feeling this and blow her girlfriend a kiss. As though she could feel it, Lexa looked over to the chief's scowl. For most, Macbay's stare terrified them. Lexa just smiled back at him and waved, undeterred by his objection. He stared at her for a fair few moments before turning to the crowd and finishing the ceremony.

Walking to her second home, housed in between the police academy and the station itself, she thought to herself 'now she was finally able to make some real changes.' It wasn't in the way she had thought, with all the training she received from Dorian. She thought she would be fighting like he did during the war. After his fourth term, Dorian decided against going back to the front line and instead took a home side position, identifying and preventing covert enemy forces from terrorizing civilians. It worked well for the most part and after a while, people began to call him 'Tempest.' Unlike Lexa however, Dorian didn't want to wear a costume to protect himself, his identity, or those around him. He felt it wasn't needed, a soldier didn't need such protection. This was mostly due to the unseen forces working with him. Soldiers, businessmen and even some politicians used what resources they had to help him. All of them agreed that Dorian needed to be the representative for the group, leaving the rest hidden. After a year of homeland defence, something happened between him and their enemy, the neighbouring country of Verthollow. This event was something Dorian would never talk about, no matter how much Lexa questioned him about it. A part of her was thankful he didn't want to share; what information could find, made her sick. A sharp breeze hit her as she walked into her new room. Twice the size of her old one at the training academy. This was emphasized by the minimised style of the room. The double bed was centred on the back wall with a night stand on either side. The only other piece of furniture in the room was a wardrobe which rested next to the feature wall opposite the door. Lexa walked passed the door to her on suite bathroom and over to the only shelf in the room. Lexa placed the flintlock rifle on the rifle stand next to her bed walked over to her wardrobe and changed from her formal cadet uniform into her own clothes. Just as she had finished there was a knock at the door. "One second," Lexa shouted out the person on the other side of the door.

"Alright, but please hurry sweetie." Kimberley answered rather quickly. Hearing who it was, Lexa dropped her uniform on the bed and walked quickly to the door. Kimberley stood in the door in an oversized brown coat. She walked in and stood in the centre of the room and took a deep breath as Lexa closed the door. "It's good there's no windows in this place." Kimberley took another deep breath in and in one quick turn on the spot, she dropped the coat to reveal what she wore underneath. A skin-tight black top with the word Police stencilled in white on the front, blue denim jeans that rested high on her waist with knee-high black boots. To finish her look off, she had deep blue and black straps around her wrists with fingerless gloves. She smiled nervously and tried her best to stand confidently, hands causally on her waist. "I just wanted to say congratulations in the best way I know how." She said softly, her voice shaking slightly. Lexa smiled at this, walked over to her and picked Kimberley up with ease. On instinct Kimberley wrapped her legs around Lexa's waist. They both smiled and kissed fiercely, Lexa's hands locking under Kimberley's legs.

"I thought I was going to meet you at the restaurant later tonight." Lexa said, the surprise in her voice going slowly. Kimberley rushed her hand through Lexa's hair and smiled back "I thought you might want to avoid the stress and skip to the end of the celebration." Lexa smiled and she moved them both to the bed.

It was a cold winters night and Lexa was slowly walking home from work. Her winter coat and scarf wrapped tightly around her neck and head with part of it drooped her face to keep herself safe from the heavy snow. She normally would have taken the bus however; all bus services had been cancelled because of the snow. A muffled shout came from behind Lexa and she turned on the spot. A blurry figure walking slowly through the blizzard. "Hey there, cutie pie."

She sprung up and out of her nightmare, memories of that night that no mattered she tried, she couldn't forget. Panic flowed through her until she looks down and saw Kimberley sleeping naked next to her. Lexa slowly laid back down stoking Kimberley's arm softly, from her shoulder down to fingertips. She smiled warmly in her sleep at her girlfriend's touch and shuffled closer. Just as she was about to fall back to sleep, there was a loud bang on the door. Lexa quickly but discreetly moved to the door, grabbing her nightgown from her end of the bed. She flung it over her head as she listened on her side of the door.

"Come on Deano, why are we bothering with her?" shouted one voice, hoarse and clearly drunk.

"Yeah, we need more of the drink and she's just going…" another voice started as Lexa opened the door. "Oh, hi" the second voice slurred and waved hazily in Lexa's direction, stumbling on the spot. He continued as though he hadn't even spoke to her, "…she'll just drag us down with her annoying face." His shouted, his voice echoing down the hallway. Lexa walked forward, pushing Dean back from the doorway, who stumbled back onto the wall opposite and down to the floor. Unconcern by this, Lexa shut the door behind her.

"What's this all about, its two in the morning." Lexa ordered with such force that it made the drunk group back away slightly.

"Ah don't mind them," Dean dismissed with a wave of his hand as he shuffled up to stand. "They're just jealous that they couldn't get your help. Hey, Hey, Lexxxxa, do you want to go for a drink?" Dean's toxic breath flooded at Lexa as he stood next to her, resting his arm over Lexa's shoulder to stabilise himself. His other hand holding a bottle of expensive mead, which sprayed its contents on the floor as Dean swayed. "See, I was telling the guys here, that you could get us into any club in town with your 'charm'." He says the last word in quotations and laughed to himself as his bottle dropped to the floor.

Lexa pushed Dean away, hard and he fell on his pair of friends who caught him, barely. Before they could repeat their drunken request, she used her power to get them to forget the reason why they were there in the first place. They looked around in a daze and wondered down the hallway that they had come from. Lexa sighed to herself and moved back in her room.

CHAPTER NINE

The end of the month had arrived far too soon for Malik and he wasn't prepared in the slightest, this was mostly due to the resignation to his father's orders. He checked his pinstriped suit in his office mirror, brushing off non-existing hairs to keep himself preoccupied. He clenched away the shake in his hand when he heard the knock on his door. He took a deep inward breath "Come in Mr Bashert, I hope we can settle this agreement quickly." His monotone voice projected as he turned around and readied himself. To his surprise and relief, it wasn't his father's lawyer but his friend and manager of the shop, Chloe. The pair were in the registration building during the Omegan attack and afterwards they got to talking about what brought them that day. When Malik heard that she was there because of her losing her job. He offered her a job in his shop, this idea was compounded when he found out about Chloe's power. "Don't worry Malik, that creepy guy hasn't come back yet. In fact, there is a person here who says she might be able to help with your problem." Chloe reassured as she walked in with a familiar face following behind.

"What are you doing here? I didn't think I'd be seeing you so soon, I'm glad you're feeling better." Malik smiled and gestured towards one of the empty chairs in front of his desk. Lexa nodded in acknowledgement as she walked in wearing her patrol uniform, a fitted royal blue suit with a Steelhaven police badge on the right side of her chest.

"I'm doing well thank you. I didn't come for a check-up however, I got a call from your friend here, it seems like you're having trouble." she said showing no worry. "It's a shame that you didn't call me sooner, it would have been dealt with already." Lexa pulled the recommended chair out and sat down. Malik was taken back by her confidence, perhaps he was too close to the situation to see the right course of action, Malik thought to himself. Thankfully, because of his power, that worry did not show on his face. Or any emotion for that matter, even his eyes were cold and blank. He had perfected this trick in the time he had been in control of his shop. It portrays confidence to his clients. Although Lexa was speaking about the various paths Malik could go down in trying to keep control of his business, he wasn't listening, instead he sat behind his desk and pretending to write down what she was advising him about. What was the point? He thought, there was no way to get around his father's orders. Even if Malik got around this obstruction, his father would just find another way around it. Having his wholesale contacts boycott the shop, most of whom hadn't fully accept Malik as the new owner. Or spread rumours about Malik's power tracker falsifying his usages to force unsuspecting customers to buy his products. These ideas, amongst a several others swam around his head as Lexa sat and explained.

"Have you even been listening?" Malik looked over his paper in confusion to an offended Lexa, he thought back to the information she was giving him then he realised. She had been countering all the possible troubles he was thinking. Malik looked her up and down and noticed something was missing.

"I didn't think you'd be able to be a police officer without a power tracker or use your ability like that. I thought your power is memory control, not telepathy." He asked, indicating at his own tracker.

"If you remember I'm able to change memories in real time. It's not much different than just reading them and to answer your first question. It would true if I were working on a case, I'm currently off duty so there's no conflict of interest. Not that it would make any difference. Sadly, the evidence I find is tarnished by my ability apparently. With there being no solid proof that I hadn't falsified the evidence. My girlfriend says there's something more to it, but I don't agree. At any rate." Lexa reached over the desk and comforted Malik "Don't worry, I have an idea about what to do." Although Malik was unconvinced by Lexa's plan, he trusted her enough to see it through.

It was late in the afternoon when Malik entered Mr Bashert's office, with Lexa following close behind. The chill in the air rushed passed them the moment the door opened. That chill continued throughout the room, from the icy blue walls to the steel columns and chairs plastered around its edges. A large central desk sat at the back wall, sat behind was a young man in a lime green suit. His style followed closely to that of his boss, who could be seen through the glass door to his office. From the matching gelled down hair to his spotless attire, making sure everything stayed in place and project the perfected appearance Mr Bashert's business was known for. The assistants' gaze was focused solely on his computer screen, not even to look up at Malik when he passed him to walk into the back office.

"Mr Cowan, I thought I told you not to disturb me today, I'm very... ah Mr Taylor, I don't see your appointment on my calendar for today, what brings you here?" Mr Bashert inquired calmly, looking up from his computer, he waved away his assistant who had stood up after the fact. "If this has anything to do with our agreement, I'm afraid that my stance on that has not changed. In fact, I have the contract already drawn up, if would be so kind to sign it, I can get back to more important work." He continued as he pulled out the contract from his desk draw, placing it on the table and gesturing for Malik to sit down. Just like his assistant outside, Mr Bashert couldn't see Lexa as she walked silently around to the side of the desk, standing on his right side. Malik sat across from Mr Bashert, staring at him and away from the contract.

"I understand that, don't worry, I'm not here to contest this. It's why I haven't brought my lawyer with me and..."

"I'm surprised you even went to an attorney, considering the conversation you had with your father." Mr Bashert interrupted. "Now, let's not draw this out for too long, I have more important things that demand my..." a sudden shiver rushed through Mr Bashert's right, his gaze sprung over. Startled, Lexa flinched away and pushed further into his mind.

"Are you alright? do you still have him?" Malik questioned.

"What did you just say?" Mr Bashert asked in a haze, mist waved around his head. He closed his eyes strongly and tried to expel this confusion. Lexa bent over and clasping her head in a severe pain. He was about to stand up to help her, when Lexa pushed him back in his chair by the shoulder and silently motioned to him to continue. His concern didn't leave him however, as Malik could see blood began to fall from Lexa's nose. Lexa roughly wiped it away and covertly switched the contract in front of Mr Bashert with the one her and Malik had brought with them. She then motioned again for him to continue, this time with more force. He sighed heavily but continued his conversation for Mr Bashert under protest.

"It's not a matter of surprise..." Malik continued. "It's just strange how both you and my father thought that I would go to him first and not anywhere else." Thankfully, this successfully brought Mr Bashert's attention back to the conversation.

"Either way, I'm glad you saw sense on this matter, now if you don't mind, sign here." Mr Bashert's cold stare returned as though nothing had happened. A small smile creped over his face as Malik picked up a pen and signed the document to finalise their business together. They both stood up with Mr Bashert passing the deed to Smith and Taylor over to Malik. With them finalising their deal by shaking hands, Malik nodded and left with Lexa following close behind.

Lexa rushed passed Malik as they left Tiberius's building, holding her right hand over her mouth, she ran across to the alleyway opposite. This wasn't like other memory change, Bashert's mind was strong, stronger than any Humankind should be, or Drem for that matter. Under normal circumstances, Lexa knew that the human mind could twisted with relative ease. Even most Drem could be altered, given enough persuasion. His mind had a strength that Lexa could not explain, nor the weakened state the whole event had put her in. She sat down next to the dumpster, away from the sightlines from the street.

"I'm so glad that worked, thank you for getting this sorted. I honestly don't know how I can thank you." Malik gratefully told Lexa, not seeing her distress until he got close enough. "Hey… are you okay?" Malik asked looking down at Lexa, her body convulsing sharply and gasping for breath. Lexa composed herself slowly with several deep inward breathes.

"You…you never told me that he had power." Lexa stated, lifting her head up weakly.

"What do you mean? He doesn't have power." Malik responded in confusion, beginning to kneel down but Lexa stopped him. Staggering to her feet, she rested her back onto the wall behind her. "If he does, it's not something he's declared." Malik continued as he pulled out his phone in trying to confirm that information. Before he could show the confirmation, he had found, there was a shout from across the street. Malik looked over to see Tiberius's assistant, Oliver Cowen, Malik rushed over to intercept him and keep him away from Lexa, whether it there was an issue with the paperwork, or the memory altercation had worn off, Lexa didn't know or care. All she could do was focus on her breathing, the pushing pain in the base of her skull made her surroundings blur together and pour a ringing down Lexa's ears, making it hard for her to stay conscious. Although she had to demand herself to stay awake, falling unconscious would reveal her to the assistant and make all that lead up to that point mean nothing. So, she focused solely on her breathing.

> A deep inhale and held for four seconds
> A deeper exhale and held for seven seconds

This was repeated until Lexa felt a force shake her shoulder, she opened her eyes slowly, hoping against hope that it was not the assistant and to her relief it was Malik. His eyes still shot with concern, which was kind of the kid, Lexa thought. She took a large breath in and could finally stood back onto her feet.
"What did he want? Did he know?" Lexa asked as she looked over to where he would have been standing.
"Thankfully not, I dropped my wallet as we rushed out." Malik replied as he rested his hand on Lexa's shoulder. She copied this action, trying her best to stabilise herself. "I don't think they saw anything, and we got what we came for, the deed." Malik gleefully told her, holding up the green, laminated piece of paper. He was so excited, finally free of an overbearing father. So happy that Malik forgot where he was and began to jump happily on the spot. The plans that had flooded Malik's mind were shattered when his eyes focused to see Lexa back on the floor. Just as he helped her back to her feet, a thunderous roar shock down the alleyway and through into the street around them. Even in her weakened state, Lexa pulled herself up straight and outstretches her hand to protect Malik from the unknown danger. The walls of the alleyway like stood in rippled like water, bending and twisting away from the source. But instead of an explosion, it withdrew back inward and out again, like the walls were breathing, with each exhale projecting out with more force. Between pulses, Lexa staggered out of the alley and onto the main street, pulling Malik back to the street and against the corner before the shock wave hit, sending an ear-piercing screech that pained all who heard it.
Lexa moved to turn back into the alley "No, don't you dare!" Malik shouted, the ringing in his ears still shaking him strong. So much so that he could not hear Lexa's reply. "Look, you need

to stay here." Malik dragged Lexa back again as it was clear she wasn't listening.

"It's far too dangerous!" Again, Lexa pulled away but now Malik was shouting.

"I need you! Everyone here needs help!" Malik gestured to the terrified people plastered along the road.

Lexa thought about it for a moment and nodded in agreement. She reached into her pocket, grabbed her phone.

It took twenty minutes for Lexa's reinforcements to arrive, that gave her enough time to recuperate. The blasts of energy and sound still ran through the streets repeatedly, pushing itself farther and farther outward. Every tremor pushed Lexa to the ground, she continued to help those around her and drove people down the open street and away from danger. This included Malik. The reinforcements arrived in a heavily armoured personal carrier, DPO printed in neon blue on either side, DPO being an acronym for Drem protection Operations, which was exclusive to be the highest trained branch of the police force that specialised in Drem related attacks. The passenger in the front jumped out and Lexa stood relived to see a friendly face.

"Detective O'hearn, what's the situation?" Asked Captain Durand, a middle aged man with short white hair and a large bushy moustache. He was one of several who marched out of the armoured police truck. Twelve officers came out of the back of the carrier, all in black full body armour which comprised mostly of Talgane, the purest form of steel on the market and a Steelhaven speciality. Most came over and surrounded Lexa with three of them moving to help the civilians flee the area. Being Lexa's firearm trainer, Captain Durand knew better than to argue Lexa's position in the upcoming firefight and passed over a matching helmet and vambrace like the rest of the DPO had on. Lexa equipped it right away, knowing that the isolated helm would protect her from the attack, but only when it had fully calibrated. A secondary function of the helm however was that it identified and helped combat powers, as she put the equipment on, a deepening set into her, like standing at the bottom of the ocean. A few seconds later the on-board computer light up and welcomed Lexa by displaying her name, rank and her badge number. Captain Durand tapped Lexa on the shoulder and passed over a plasma rifle, the modern weaponry of the police force, powered by plasma core at its base. Lexa breathed in deeply and looked down to the source of the attack. The computer automatically identified and extrapolated all the information it could. The blue heads-up display showed that the source was over a mile away located at the large cathedral on the borders of the industrial district. The building stood strong and the attack was projected in rings outward. The attack had rolled out for over two miles so far. Lexa and the rest of the group stood facing the source with Durand holding his hand over his computerized vambrace. Another shock wave rippled towards them, the moment it hit the Durand pressed a button in unison to identify the frequency of the sound. It rippled through the air but only could be heard for a fraction of a second before it vanished.

"What's the plan Captain?" Lexa asked as she turned around.

"We are Delta squad, there are twelve other squads arranged at different locations." Durand replied indicating the locations on the spike projector housed in his vambrace. "We're going to advance down specified paths until we get to the centre and secure the situation." The rest of the groups were collected at the opening of the alleyway and marched down ready to fight. It was a strange sensation, to be able to hear all around and yet see the ongoing vibration attack churned around them with no affect on them. As they got closer to centre this attack could be felt, like a long hum that rippled in the floor as they marched. The gunfire could barely be heard, even when Lexa moved around the corner and saw the carnage.

The Deven'ra cathedral stood on top of the largest hill in Steelhaven, the cathedral's foundations had been carved out of the hill itself, so that the high priest that lived inside could watch over the city. The upper floor was made of the purest Talgane. The roof had seven spires sprouted to the sky with the central spire housing a statue of Deven'ra herself. There were entrances on all four sides and in front of the eastern entrance stood a statue of Deven'ra's successor, Wui. This was the start of a line of statues of successors that spiralled down and around the building, concluding with Apothus. Who, in the lore, used a slither of his heart to create the Drem'onor. Although a rival belief is that Apothus was a demon that created cursed beings to destroy the purity of Humankind. A blur of flame twisted around the outskirts of the cathedral, swirling through the status of Deven'ra's successors. The spiral of steel statues, the upper floors of the cathedral shown like stars stuck to the ground. Lexa had to close her eyes for a moment while her helmet adjusted to the blinding light. The fire shield in a dome shape gave the attackers a regenerative shield that kept them safe from the police fire. However, that did not stop the Drem attackers from passing though untouched by its heat. Lexa and her squad rushed forward and took refuge behind the large stone display with a painting of Deven'ra with the caption 'Welcoming with the healing light of Goddess'. Lexa looked down at her vambrace to see the computer had connected with the others in the squads around the square. The projection, showed the separate squads probing the shield for any weakness.

"This isn't going to work," Lexa shouted to Durand, forgetting that she doesn't need to.

"What do you mean? We have to find a weak spot to push through." Durand replied, gesturing towards his squad to make a defensive wall. Lexa grabbed Durand's arm before he could move with them.

"And that would be fine, if there wasn't an Aerokinetic controlling the wind to keep the fire moving." Lexa informed him.

"There's no indicators of people controlling the wind," Durand countered as he lifted his arm, but before he could look down at it, a burst of fire shot across the back of their cover, shaking it slightly.

"Look, just trust me." Lexa replied, her voice shaking in her fright. It was one thing to practise in a safe space, but the reality is very different. Like she did just after her interaction with Bashert, Lexa closed her eyes and concentrated on her breathing for a few seconds. As the world closed of around her, she noted Durand begin to discuss the best course of action with the other squad leaders at the other exit points. The fire shield breathed slowly, growing with every inhale. Lexa stretched out with her power and felt the groups fighting. The DPO gunning down the attackers, their rifles held the range over their opponents. The Drem found a way around this however, by retreating into their shield and drawing them into rushing out of their cover.

"I need you to track and shout out their locations, we're getting overrun." Durand ordered, panic hiding far in his voice. Before Lexa could respond, Durand was up and back on his feet and shouting orders to the rest. Lexa returned to her meditation and noted three Cryokinetics coming from the north, holding large ice spikes in both hands. Their frost channelled up their forearms to their elbows. Another three groups from the west, from the direction of the cathedral, throwing and regenerating their ice spikes as they advanced. Lexa estimated that there were at least one Terrakinetic as large blocks formed from the ground as her side tried to counter their attacks. This was strange to her, as no other squad had reported such an ability happening around them. She relayed this information to Durand who then repositioned his forces accordingly to the threats. Slowly, Lexa's fear began to subside as the squad established a stable defensive point. Durand rushed over to Lexa, who was about to congratulate him on his leadership when. "I need you to spearhead a press in the dead zone and get a closer look at their shield for any signs of weakness, we have a handle on their current tactics. Here take Samson, Brill and Chester with you." Lexa had been volunteered without saying a word and now three towering DPO officers stood over her. With a quick check of nervous, Lexa gestured towards the cathedral and they began their approach.

The ground was scorched, and dust roamed thickly around their shins, the team marched into the dead zone. Even the attacking Drem were wary to stay for too long in this area as there was little cover in the gap between the two defensive lines. They shifted along the line of raised ground that the attackers had previously made. This became more difficult the further they ventured in as the cover became scarce. Lexa followed the tallest of her group, Chester, while she continued her analysis of the enemy's movements. Drem had stopped advancing from directly ahead and instead focused their attention on the sections on either side, hoping to take control of those areas and flank Durand and his team from both sides. Lexa smiled at this, if she able to push further, she thought to herself. Then she could end this whole situation quickly. Just ahead was their final visible cover, a small cave that the Terrakinetics must have created to create overhead cover, in case the air support. The hurricane like winds from the shield, kept them at bay. She was so focused on monitoring for the enemy that she didn't notice that Chester had stopped in front of her until she had walked into him.

"Report!" Lexa commanded as she lifted up her gun ready, worried about an unknown hostile, Chester muttered something quietly before spinning around unexpectedly and smashing the butt of his gun into Lexa's forehead, knocking her unconscious.

The other two squad members moved closer and knelt over Lexa's unconscious body, each placing an object hidden on her. Brill wrapped a small explosive along Lexa's right hip, hidden behind her holstered side arm. Samson clipped on a micro camera on top of Lexa's badge and linked it with his computerised vambrace.

"This doesn't feel right sir, she's protected us this far and we're just going to turn on her?" Samson questioned.

"We have our orders," Chester demanded, the booming nature of his voice hiding his own uncertainty about Durand's plan. "Take up defensive positions there and there and get ready to move when I say." He pointed towards the opening leading towards the enemy, the light of the shield was focused through the opening. All three of them took their assigned positioned and readied their weapons.

Lexa opened her eyes and for a moment, she thought that was safe at home. The smoke and dust from the shield brought her back to reality. Blasts of plasma fire echoed far in the distance, but as Lexa stood up, she noticed something strange. There was a warm maroon glow all around her with small flakes of fire falling from the sky. She tracked the shield wall in front of her, that for some reason was protruding inward, that confusion left her, as her gaze reached the ceiling, she realised she was inside the dome and sitting on the steps of the cathedral. A low tremor began underneath her, Lexa looked around in a panic until her gaze feel on the cathedral entrance. Standing in unison were two parallel lines of the attackers that ran up the stairs. Each of the enemy combatant were covered in tribal tattoos that glowed Azure blue under the light of the shield, the tattoos continued onto their armour, which wasn't much unlike the DPO's armour with some notable differences. The Cryokinetics' armour was lighter without any on their arms, which was covered in their power. The Terrakinetic used their power to cover their chest and left shoulder with smooth rock to protect them with the rest covered in Talgane. Both types of armour were lighter, giving more freedom to move. Each one of them had more tattoos depending on their rank. The leader of the group stood larger than the rest, unlike like his subordinates, he was covered with heavier armour from head to heel. The paint plastered over it beamed so brightly, it looked almost angelic. From his back protruded large crystal spikes sprayed in the shape of a pair of wings. The wings beamed a white light over Lexa.

"Ah, yet another traitor to their kind, you scramble around the shoes of the weak, substituting your greatness for cowardice. How do you explain your presence here?" The leader's voice seemed to project right into Lexa's ear and yet far off in the distance, she flinched in surprise. The others began to chant a single word, "Zham, Zham, Zham, Zham." The leader began to walk down to Lexa, she tried to stand up to better defend herself. This idea was quickly dashed away by the enemy to her left, who lifted his hand and sunk her down into to the floor. Creating a small rounded platform and lifted her in the air. She was then shifted against her will to her knees, with her hands secure in the ground behind her. "You don't move unless we allow you to." The leader, Zham, Lexa presumed, continued walking, patting the shoulder of his comrade as he walked by. While Zham was walking towards, Lexa finally realised that the tremor wasn't coming from the group in front of her, but from the explosive device on her hip. A standard issue plasma grenade, that would shoot out a beam of pure energy, the realisation of this made her freeze to the spot. Zham stopped and the vibration subsided, which aloud Lexa to relax slightly. The others around him prepared their frost weapons. Instead of readying them for attack, the began to knock them together in unison. Again, and again, increasing in speed, but all Lexa could do was stare at Zham. She had no idea what would set the explosive off, but she estimated that it had something to do with his movement. "What do you see when you look out there?" The leader questioned as he moved passed Lexa, The Terrakinetic in the group twisted her platform so that the pair were both facing outward. "Because what I see is weakness, the weakness of a system holding our people down."

Lexa said nothing, her mind was too preoccupied, all she could think about was finding a way to get this device off her. This didn't seem to matter to Zham as he continued, "But imagine if there was a better way, a purer way. We, the Nephilim, have that way, we wish to get rid of these disgusting creatures and give the freedom that all Drem'onor deserve. To use your power as and when you pleased. I'm sure you've felt that and why not? It's not like those creatures wouldn't choose the same way if they were in our position." There was nothing she could do to inspect the device; any movement would be countered by the zealot behind her. The only thing she could do would be to check her memories to find a way. The fighting outside the shield was roaring harsher than ever, blasts of plasma shoot against the barrier that would instantly vanish. Lexa closed her eyes. "Therein lies the problem though, they aren't in our situation. We are the ones with the power after all and that frightens them. We are their betters and they..." Zham trailed off from his rhetoric as he saw Lexa. Before she could react, Zham's hand was pressed firmly against her shoulder. In that split second between that and the reaction of the explosion, Lexa tore away something vital. Flashes of violent colours and sounds which swam through her brain like fire. Visions of something being crystallized in the streets, streams of flags with a set of crystal wings flapped in the breeze. A subtle speech ran through it all, though barely above a whisper, it somehow stood out above all others, with all one word recognisable 'Fear'.

A spray of black energy blasted out from the shield in front of him, piercing a tear inside wide enough to pass through. Durand knew that his plan had worked. He smiled to himself as he stood up and shouted the command to charge, there was no telling how long they had this opportunity for, and he wasn't going to waste it. As the officers in front of him pushed through the tear, Durand heard shots of gunfire with little sounds of retaliation. Durand sped up and pushed through the gap, running as though he ran through water to get to the other side. What was on the other side, he hadn't planned for. Surrounding the cathedral was yet another shield, like the previous one, it had the exact same shape tear running through its side. There were several Drem attackers still standing in between them and the primary shield.

Durand assessed the battlefield to see a group of Aerokinetics and Pyrokinetics sitting in a circle on two points next to the shield. He ordered for his men to attack them as he rushed forward. Steams of frost spikes shoot passed him, but he didn't stop. Only when he got to the foot of the stairs to the cathedral did he even slow down. The source of the blast stood just under the first step, as he rested next to it, he saw the remnants of Lexa, her right side frayed almost burnt to a crisp. "I'm sorry" Durand whispered under his breath, then pushed on to enter the building.

It was empty, no hostile Drem or civilians in sight. He did not understand, intelligence from his commanders indicated that there were hostiles inside holding at least fifty hostages, one of whom being the high priest of Deven'ra. Panic rushed over Durand as he searched the building with his computerised vambrace, sending out a sonic locator to find someone, anyone inside. Even if that someone was a hostile, anything to justify what he had just done. When it came up empty, Durand fell to his knees and wept, he had ordered the death of a child for nothing, he tears turned to anger. He sprang up to his feet and screamed with such force that it echoed down to the alter at the opposite end.

The doors behind him swag open and two more officers rushed in, Chester and Brill

"Sir, what do you have?" Chester barked as they both moved into cover, Durand didn't reply. After checking that the coast was clear, the pair moved over to their commanding officer. "We have a situation out here sir," Chester said as he tapped Durand on the shoulder. What did it matter? Durand thought to himself, he had done the unforgivable. This remorse vanished as soon as he heard what the situation was.

Lexa was still alive.

When Kimberley first got there, Lexa's pain was nothing to the fear felt towards the doctors. Kimberley walked in on Lexa holding back the healer's hands shouting, "don't you touch me" and "get away" as loud as her lungs would allow her. Lexa pulled back with her good hand and landed a strike across the healer's jaw, which knocked them out. It took over an hour of Kimberley trying to calm her down before she would allow them anywhere near her. Kimberley understood the reason why, she also understood how much pain she must have been in. Her legs had been shattered into pieces, held together only by burnt flesh. The singed flesh travelled up to engulf her entire right side and both shoulders. Lexa's face was gone, the blast had hit her face with such force that her right eye was gone, leaving her cheekbone and temple exposed. Her right ear was also gone, and the bridge of her nose had been shaven down to almost nothing. Kimberley sat next to Lexa's left and held her hand.

"Tell me what happened sweetie," was the only reassuring words Kimberley could say before the Healer had tried again to heal her face, but Lexa pushed them away. "I'm hoping that situation with Malik could be resolved." Kimberley said, bringing Lexa's focus back on her.

"Yeah, he was able to get back the deed to his business. But that wasn't what put me in here, they turned on me, the bastards. They knocked me unconscious and left me to be a Drem bomb. I'm going to kill them!" Lexa screamed, anger rushing through her as she gripped Kimberley's hand tightly. The healing light washed over Lexa's face, repairing it with every second. It didn't take long for the healer to regrow her eye, some of her nose and a portion of her ear. She winced in pain and pushed the healer away "Get out!" Lexa screamed repeatedly at the Healer, who rushed out of the room as a bedpan was thrown at her.

"Sweetie please, you must be in so much pain. All we want to do is help you." Kimberley softly spoke as she holds Lexa's left hand.

"It's not that simple and you know it, why should I trust them, any of them." Lexa snapped as she pulled her hand away. "I need to get away from them, I need my freedom."

"I thought you had be in the police for at least two years before you could leave?" Kimberley asked, trying to calm her girlfriend down, she lightly pulled Lexa's hand back and stroked it softly. "What they did was wrong I know, but you could always go through the proper channels and bring them to justice, Internal affairs will help you."

"What I need is to enlist, I'll try your way and go to IA. But I'm going to demand that they move me to the army. They almost killed me, regardless of their intent." Kimberley's eyes glazed cold and the grip in her hand went. Lexa would be gone for at least four years, if she survived at all. With recent border disputes happening in the west and now this new group, the Nephilim. There was no hope that Lexa would survive the first six months, let alone her for term of service. Kimberley voiced those concerned but it didn't change her mind. So, she kissed Lexa on the forehead, and she left, her eyes filled with tears.

That night was the hardest for Kimberley to cope, she got into bed as soon as she got home. She lay there crying for hours, she had lost the love of her life and know she lost all desire for the future. As she slowly fell asleep her dream told a different story of how that afternoon happened.

The mist flowing through her dream made it difficult to understand, she could recognise the important parts. Walking into Lexa's hospital room Kimberley was expecting the worst, from the reports. Only to find Lexa's injuries were almost completely gone. She sat upright in her bed and calming discussing her treatment with the healer that was finishing healing her wounds. When she noticed Kimberley, Lexa smiled. "Hey there, how are you doing?"

"How am I doing?" Kimberley asked astonished "You're the one who had this done to you." Lexa laughed at this.

"I'll be alright sweetie; the healers are the finest in the city," Lexa reassured as she passed over her lunch plate as the healer got up to leave the room. "Now, before you tell me that I shouldn't take this lying down, don't worry, I've handled it." Lexa then went on to tell her a story that shifted in and out of focus. "... I smashed my fist into Durand's face then I moved onto..." as much as Lexa was enjoying telling Kimberley how she got her revenge, Kimberley cuts her off.

"Honey, don't you think that you took that a bit too far?" she asked, with an unamused look on her face.

The dream mist roared over the scene to reveal Lexa dressed and sitting on her hospital bed discussing with Kimberley as she sat down next to her.

"I need you to listen to me because this is important. With of the new group revealing taking action against the capital. Some of the Captains at work believe that an investigation needs to be started. It'll cover all companies and/or parties involved."

"Why is that sweetie?" the concern in Kimberley's voice making it shake slightly.

"It's difficult to explain right now, what's important is that I'll be a part of the investigation." Before Kimberley could raise her concerns, Lexa continued. "I have to go undercover in the Omegans, the higher ups believe that The Nephilim have psychic influence over them, so they can sow discourse to gain a foothold in Steelhaven. They also believe, and I agree, that my power would be a great asset in bringing a peaceful end to it all quicker." Lexa reached out and held both of Kimberley's hands and explained her plans in its entirety.

PART TWO

CHAPTER ONE

Out of all the regions of Steelhaven, from the farming district to the south to the military and law enforcement districts to the north, there breed distrust between Humankind and Drem. Where that hate stood most prominent was in Ulton, the factory district, which for the past fifty years it slowly moved to be solely inhabited by Humankind. At first it was explained away by the factories employing more Humankind over the years. "Giving power to the powerless." That was the slogan that hid the prejudice that grow in strength through the streets. Over time that slogan faded away, but the seperation remained intact. So, when the news broadcast about over a hundred organisations would be investigated for ties with Nephilim. There was uproar all throughout Steelhaven, from both Humankind and Drem, but nowhere more pronounced than in The Red Jackal, Ulton's only public house. The occupants of the night the news was released, began to plan a riot. One of the front runners of the mob was a young man named Maxwell Conroy, a seventh generation foundry worker. He and a few others shouted their rhetoric from on top of the bar. Over the night the mob slowly dispersed, which wasn't noticed until the alcohol had subsided. It was two o'clock in the morning and Max jumped off the counter, chugged the last of his pint and slammed it down for another. He looked up, swaying on the spot as the barman blurred in and out of focus. "I'm going to have to cut you off sonny, you've had enough." The barman instructed, grabbing the glass off Max which caused him to slam his forehead into the bar. He grunts in pain, shook his head violently from side to side, and swipes to get his glass back but misses and falls to the floor. A large roar of applause came from the bar as Max drew all their attention, especially the high tables in the VIP section. Unlike most of the bar, which was covered in brown leather and stained wood. The VIP section was raised up in the corner, opposite the bar. It was created out of black marble. The area only had two tables with their chairs edged into the wall, quilted in black leather and facing outward to have an overview of the building. There sat a group of ten, six men and four women. Wearing matching tailored, black suits under large, black overcoats. Stitched in their right breast pocket was the symbol of The Omegans. It rested small and hidden from view, but it was there for those who knew where to look. The group had paired up, each having their own distinct conversations. One of the pair stopped their conversation and watched the drunk stubble back to his feet.

"Who's the loudmouth down at the bar Donna?" One of the men asked the woman to his right. He was a man in his fifties, with a short crew cut and cleanly shaven face. He sat hunched forward and rested his flagon of ale with in his right hand back on the table. He outstretched that and pointed down towards Max. "I haven't seen him around here before."

"If I remember rightly Darnall, his name is Maxwell Conroy. He recently lost his job, working over at Shiny Rock with those two." Donna replied as she pointed over to a pair in the corner of the bar, sleeping. Unlike Darnall, Donna Shinecroft sat small but powerful, her shoulders pulled back as strongly as her hair which was high into a bun. She looked down her nose at the drunk, smirking at the man steadying himself on one of his friends. "I wouldn't give him too much attention right now, we have more pressing matters to concern ourselves with." Donna tapped Darnall's arm three times and placed her hand back on the map sitting in front of them. The map of Steelhaven was splashed with numerous coloured flags. She calmly moved several of them from the registration district off the map and moved several other groups to various parts of the city, explaining her movements as she did. "In the past four months since the Nephilim attack the cathedral, there's been over a dozen attacks from them and we can barely keep up." Donna continued as she moved seven groups of gold, white and blue stamps from the rows of houses surrounding the church, the city hospital and the police academy. "Now, we've been trying to keep ahead of the attacks with pre-emptive strikes. We know that we lose close quarters fights with them almost all the time." Donna then placed some gold stickers back on the outskirts of where she had taken them from. "Rotating sniper attacks on possible threats seem to keep them at bay, while we prepare." Before Darnall could respond with his own strategies, a shadow washed over the map.

"Hey, what do you got there?" a voice echoed from above them that drew the attention of everyone in the VIP section. Max smiled up at the group, swaying on the spot and downing a pint that he had clearly stolen.

"Nothing that concerns you. Now move away, this is none of your business!" Darnall barked loudly as he stood up, his bulking physique only taller than Max because of the raised platform of the VIP section. Max just beamed a wide smile back down at him, which bleed into a laugh. Darnall was disgusted by this, to be disrespected by a no one. Like he had no idea who he was talking to, Mitchell Darnall had fought for Humankind since before this little child was a twinkle in his father's eye. With a decisive swipe of his arm, Darnall stroke Max hard across the face, causing him to buckle over and spray blood across the steps. Just as he turned his back on Max, the laugh returned behind him. He spun around to see Max standing right in front of him, a mad gleam in his eyes. As Darnall lifted his arm to strike again, Max rushed forward and grabbed his arm. His grip held him in place, Max eyes seemed to burn gold as he stared back. "I've been fighting in this war for most of my life. I fought in the Verthollow war, against the Green Fire of the Seven, against the Forgotten King and the army of the never were. So, when I tell you to leave, you leave!" Darnall commanded with all the fury and might he could muster. This command drew the attention of everyone in bar, some retreated out of instinct. Max however, was too drunk to recognise the man.

Max's smiled faulted slightly as did his grip, which gave Darnall the opportunity he needed. In one smooth motion, Darnall pulled the boy across the velvet rope that divided them and slammed him onto the table behind. The rest of Darnall's group sprang up to their feet, all except Donna who didn't move an inch. She peered down at Max, who was knocked unconscious. Donna crossed her arm and checked him over in fascination. After which, she looked up at Darnall glaring down. She clicked her fingers to get his attention.

"Take him down to the basement." Donna instructed coldly.

"Are you serious?" Darnall replied frustrated, when this didn't change her expression. Darnall sighed and nodded to her "Alright, I'll take him down and kill him myself." He grabbed Max's feet and dragged him down the VIP stairs and towards the door behind the bar.

The next morning's hangover hit Max like a sledgehammer, he blinked his eyes open for a second to see white-hot light shooting down at him. He rolled on to his side, only to be stroke hard in the ribs. His cry of pain was swept away by the screams of the crowd around him. "Why must you be so loud?" Max questioned in barely more than a whisper, covering his eyes with his right arm.

"Rise and shine sleeping beauty, time to get up." Declared a voice as a pair of arms pull him up onto his feet. Max slowly opened his eyes to be greeted by a sea of bright lights, as his vision focused, he saw that he was surrounded by a ten-foot-tall cage with a dark figure standing on the opposite side. A strike to Max's stomach took the wind out of him along with the meal that he enjoyed the night before. This was celebrated by the crowd who cheered loudly. "Better out than in, here you'll need this." A voice shouted over the crowd and pushed an object into Max's stomach again. He held back the gift away this time, trying to keep something down. He looked down and focused on what it was. A Bo staff, he placed the right end on the floor and began to rest against to try and get some more sleep. This hope was dashed when it was kick out from under him. "Now, now, none of that. We need you awake for this fight." Max looked over to the person standing next to him as he knelt down and picked up the staff. "Unless you want to die that is." The man chuckled as he watched Max ache though a stretch, arching his back firmly.

"What's this all about? I don't remember much of last night, the last thing I remember I was finishing off my pre-drinks on the way to The Red Jackal, where am I?"

"Oh, you're still at The Red Jackal, you just pissed off the wrong person." The man passed over a glass of water which Max sipped it and throw the rest behind him, along with the glass. "At least he was nice enough to wait until you were awake."

"Yeah, I feel so privileged," Max finalised as he staggered forward with the staff outstretched in front of him.

"I'm Grent Agnarsson by the way" the man offered. 'Whatever' Max thought to himself, like that helped in any way.

Unlike Max, who could barely stand. Darnall was full of fire and ready to fight. He stretched his arms out as he walked towards Max, arching his own staff over his head and cracking his neck on both sides. 'A few strong strikes across his chest would end him quickly,' Darnall thought to himself. With how he was moving so heavily, it was easy for him to do before his opponent had any chance to react. Max heaved as he tried to keep himself upright. Whether it was chance or instinct Max however. In a flash of movement, he had lifted his staff to counter Darnall's strike with such force that it knocked that staff out of his hand. Max had then grabbed Darnall's exposed arms, twisted his whole body around, and dragged Darnall over his shoulder, slamming him on the ground. Silenced fell in the arena, all except Grent who let out his own cheer. Even though he was safe, Max was just grateful that the fight was over so quickly. He sat down next to Darnall's unconscious body.

"Nice one mate, didn't think you had it in you." Grent congratulated, slapping Max across the back. Grent looked around to see that the rest of the crowd, who were shouting their revulsion and pushing forward to grab them. Grent grabbed his new friend up and whispered. "We best move, no doubt they want to finish the job."

"I wouldn't go anywhere if I were you," a voice echoed across the entire room as the pair went to leave. They looked up to the north wall to see the same group from last night, with Donna the forerunner. She held her chin high as she watched the pair squirm to stop moving. "I wouldn't be too impressed with yourself however, your confidence has kept you alive this far. But it won't last much longer." She told them as she gave a signal with her hand. Within seconds there were dozens of white dots all over the pair. Seeing this, Grent put with his hands high in the air.

"My lady, this does not seem fair." He argued, a strong quiver in his voice. "I was under the impression that this bout was set up to test this guy's skills more than restoring Commander Darnall's honour?" Grent gestured towards his unconscious superior. "Deven'ra knows he has enough," Grent whispered to himself.

"That's an awfully big assumption little man, perhaps we should throw you in with this child." A scream echoed around the room, the pair turn around to see Darnall on his feet and walking towards them. They tried to back away, but it was no use as two members of the crowd had stealthy walked up behind them and grabbed them tightly under the arms. "Take them down to the holding cells! Now!" Darnall commanded, the rage in his voice overpowering Donna's own orders from above as he repeated the last word as they are dragged out of the arena.

CHAPTER TWO

Kimberly had been sitting in her car outside the community centre for over an hour. Normally, she would go in without issue. Inside was the monthly meet up for Sternberg's victims that had begun several months after his arrest. It was originally started by Lexa, who slowly convinced the rest to meet and support one another through their shared trauma. When the first meeting came about however, Lexa had an appointment with a patient and couldn't make it, so Kimberley went in her place. The next meeting, she was out of town so again Kimberley, feeling more out of place. The list of excuses continued, getting worse and until Kimberly decided that she wouldn't need to be asked to go, she just went. Now that she and Lexa had broken up however, she had missed every meeting since. That month's meeting was different, and she needed their advice. What are they going to say about her absence though and how is she going to explain it, were the many thoughts floating through her head. The pain began to swell in her chest at the thought of having to put that moment into words, tears began to fall and when she felt them, all ideas of going in left her and she turned the key in the ignition. It was in that moment when a knock of the window that startled her and caused her to stall her car. "If you're off to get a good drink, you shouldn't do so alone. I know all the best places." Olivia Graves, a slender woman just about to meet her twenties, she had long and curly black with streaks of turquoise running through. She smiled through the car window. Before Kimberley could respond, Olivia had run eagerly ran around the car and got into the passenger seat. "So, where are we going? The Wind vale is always good on a Friday night, although that might be because of ladies' night, I'm no lady but you can get my drinks for me, so it's all good." she stated excitingly as she put on her seatbelt, not noticing Kimberley's anxiety until after. "You alright?" Olivia tried to rest her hand on Kimberley's, but she moved it away. Kimberly felt streaks of tears fall on her face as she shook her head, she cleared her throat softly and recited the moments leading up to her lost love. When she had finished, Olivia gave her a hug and offered to go in explain. "It's only so they don't have to ask, it's not something you need to explain if you don't want to." Olivia interjected as she could see her friend about to refuse the offer. Kimberley instead, nodded slightly and mouthed 'thank you,' feeling too nervous to actually voice those words.

She left it a few moments before she went in. The community house sat more like a church than anything, with high wooden ceilings and several prayer rooms off to the side. There were nine chairs all placed in a circle and all facing each other. She was also met by a sea of concerned faces, which flooded her with anxiety as they beckoned her to sit down and join them. She did so, looking down at the hands instead of them, what they must be thinking, letting their champion go to such a horrible place. Even Kimberly knew of the old stories before the war, of how the Drem that joined the army were treated while they served. The way they were held down in every possible way. By the end of their term of service, The Drem that survived were broken beyond repair, refusing to use their abilities for any reason. Time had changed since the war's end, but that did not stop the rumours from continuing to spread. But there was no reasoning Lexa out of her decision, she had always been a strong-willed woman even when they were children. Once she had made up her mind, that was the end of it. Kimberley had been so lost in thought that she didn't notice Ben Westbourne had walked over and sat next to her. Ben had always been a good friend to her and he had come far from their first meeting. It was the very first meeting and he was the only other one their, he sat on his seat shaking with fear, rocking back and forth to comfort himself. Kimberley was surprised by this sight as Ben was a professional Rugby player. To see him so terrified was unsettling, Kimberley sat in the seat next to him and did her best to comfort him, considering she couldn't connect with his trauma it wasn't much, but it did help.

Kimberley looked over to him and smiled warmly, she was very grateful for the return of that help. He smiled back and he went back to his designated seat. One by one the group sat around, with David Murray, a young boy of ten to make the usual drinks for the group. As they all sat down, Kimberley noted, as she always had done, the empty chair to her right. It was an honorary place for Selina Gordon, a retiree that Sternberg had stabbed as she opened her door to him, thinking he was a salesman. Like the rest in the group, Selina had been healed by the monster and with no substantial evidence to even find Sternberg, he was able to get away scot-free. Unlike the rest however, who could share their memories with Lexa and find some remnants of peace. The mere act of this transference was more than her eighty-five year old body could cope with. Thankfully Lexa used Selina's memories, as well as the rest of the group to push justice onto the monster who had attacked them.

After they had gotten their usual drinks, the meeting begun. One by one they would tell the group whatever was on their mind, from personal to professional, political or religious, nothing held off limits. Usually Kimberley would be the third in the line-up, after Gavin and Ben. However, they decided for that meeting to 'change things up' and place Kimberley in the middle. They wouldn't say it, but she knew the reason. Many had some good news, Gavin had been promoted from Team Leader to Production Manager at the steel mill where he worked called

Shiny Rock. Olivia had graduated from art college as well as sold her first piece of art. An oil painting of Finrax, a skeletal figure draped in gold cloth with a silver rope wrapped around its waist; shrouded in black and several shades of dark purple. This made Kimberley smile, not just because her friend had finally finished college but that first that her first painting that she sold was that the God of death. 'Because how could it have been anything else?' Kimberley thought to herself as she looked over Olivia's tattoos, most devoted to Finrax, symbolic or abstract. As well as a new one on her left wrist, a thick black line twist around the inside to the inside of her wrist like the roots of a tree, they splintered out and meet just under her palm to form a tree truck and branches which melted into crow feathers. Kimberley knew what that tattoo meant, unlike Olivia's other tattoos, that all had personal meanings, the rooted feathers was a symbol of the Sect of Finrax, a 'religion' that started just after the war.

"When did you join the Sect of Finrax?" Kimberley stated out of the blue, which shocked herself more than everyone else. She brought her hand up to her mouth "Sorry," she blurted out before finding her voice again. "It's just that, with them attacking people in the street and worse, I just didn't think you would be okay with joining them."

"I can understand you worries Kimmi," Olivia started, sounding as though she had recited this for too many people already, this made Kimberley shift uneasily in her chair. "But those actions were at response of the old guard, the Sect of Finrax have evolved since then and we would never do those kinds of actions again. We are less about causing death and more about celebrating their transition to a higher plane as well as their lives leading to that point." Olivia had been retelling examples of the good works the Sect had done over the next twenty minutes, when she saw the look of Kimberley's face and realised her mistake. "I'm sorry," Olivia laughed nervously, "I've been getting a lot of people being judgemental about my decision."

"Although it does mean that you get to do more research into the acts of the Sect," Kimberley finished, which cause both Olivia and Ben laughed.

"This is true" Olivia replied, raising her cup towards her. "Now it's your turn, I hear you had an interesting night with your friend Sargent Black." As always, a silence fell over the group at the mention of Dorian. They all turned to look at Kimberley, some not as subtle as they would like. Her smile faded as she took a deep breath and started the story that brought her back to her second family.

"Within the couple of weeks since Lexa and I broke up." The pain crept out of Kimberley's voice at the mention of her ex-girlfriend's name, but she did her best to push through. "Dorian had taken upon himself to visit me every Wednesday and Friday. To see how I was coping, I believe was his exact phasing. His first visit was a strange one, my manager and I were in a rather heated debate on whether my tour in Verthollow would go on as planned. The heartbreak was too close for me and I felt that would reflect in my performance. I don't think he understood this however, as he just repeated his argument again, with more force. 'Yes, yes, I understand, but your fans have paid good money to see you sing live. You'd be letting down a lot of people. Don't throw away your career over some selfish bitch.' The last part was not part of his original argument however and in reaction to this, I slapped him, well tried to. Dorian had entered the room without either of us noticing and used his power to stop me. It was scary for a moment, did my manager have a power and never told me. It was only when I looked around for better explanation, did my fear subside. My manager must have had the same train of thought because he sighed with relief just after I did. Dorian didn't have to inform my manager of his desire to speak with me privately, he simply bowed to Dorian and left without saying a word. Dorian must have heard our fight, because he was more convincing. He reminded me that few people get to follow their dreams and succeed and that I should push through the pain as it's the only way to get past it."

"How was the tour in Verthollow by the way? I hear that the place isn't very nice," Olivia inquired, as tactfully as she could. Like the rest of the group, Olivia had only heard rumours about their sister state, seeing as there was little traffic between the two nations.

"That would be an understatement, you see. Unlike here, where the clear division between Humankind and Drem, to keep the entire population safe." Kimberley clarified, with some in the group nodding in agreement. "Their divide is all to boil the Drem right down to their power and nothing. They must use them constantly and are often beaten if they complain." In the corner of her eye, Kimberley could see small flakes of light fall and twist, she closed her mouth tight in realisation that she had said too much.

David Murray, one of the group that had power, the others being Selina, who had Gyrokinesis, or gravity manipulation, as well as Michael and Thomas' Cryokinetic. David's power was that of teleportation. He fidgetted in his seat, which only increased the light surrounded him. "David, are you okay?" Kimberley asked concerned. It wasn't clear whether he was nodding, or it was the shake that had slowly increased since the very start of the meeting itself. Before anyone could show their own concern, David had vanished, leaving a pillar of swirling white light in his wake. It shown through the base of his chair to the floor and up passed the ceiling, Kimberley looked up at the highest point of the light. She slowly looked down to see that a second pillar had appeared over in the canteen, where David stepped out. He slowly picked up another cup from the table in front of him and returned to his seat through the light. Both beacons blinked away in that instant. A silence went through the group, broken by Kimberley continued her story, quietly at first and negating the specifies she had planned for Verthollow. How in Dorian's second visit, he took her and her backing group to the market place to show them all the native produce. She left out an interaction between her and a stall owner, who he had stricken his Pyrokinetic Drem in broad daylight. The young boy had not been more than seven, by Kimberley's guess. With his small frame and hunched posture, the boy must had already stopped growing. This was mostly due to the nature of his job, which to provide a continuous heat for the wok stationed above. This is so the proprietor could sell his large portions of chicken, beef and lamp joints, all smothered in several spices that she couldn't even begin to pronounce. As she and her group got closer, the smell of the spices became intoxicating. All she knew was that they imbued the meat with a deep amethyst colour and a fiery aftertaste. The pyrokinetic had been laying on his back, pressing his hands and feet to the top of his box since the market day had started, six hours before. So, when the owner looked down at the wok in front of him and noticed that the water inside had come off the boil. The man screamed, which shocked Kimberley and the group. He ripped up his side of the cloth covering his stall, grabbed the young boy around the neck with his large, greased hand and pulled the boy up at shoulder height, screamed something loudly in his face and hit the body in the stomach with such force that the boy's legs curled up to protect himself. As though they were of one mind, Kimberley quickly reached over and pulled the child towards her to protect him. At the same moment, Dorian used his power to hold the owner away from the pair. Dorian pulled the man towards him to put in his place, only for Kimberley to step in and scream how wrong this was and how he should be ashamed of himself. When she was finished, not only did she notice the scared look on the man's face, but that everyone around her had fell deathly silent. She turned to fall back into her group. One by one, her friends started clapping and cheering, with Dorian stepping forward and patting her on the back. Thankfully, Dorian's other visits were less eventful, so she could tell them in their entirety. It was last night that Kimberley had finally plucked up enough courage to ask Dorian something she had been wondering since their fourth outing.

"Was that he was trying to get into your pants? Because that's what I would do." Olivia asked confidently, not realising what she had said. The rest of the group spun around to stare at her. "What?" she asked confused. David started laughing first, softly as he did most things, he brought his hand up to his mouth to hide her smile, that laughter soon spread through half of the group before Olivia finally understood. "No, no, no." She repeated and stood up, her hand stretched out. "That's not what I meant, it was just obvious that he was hitting her, and I would tell him to stop it…shut up!" She shouted as she strode over to the canteen, mostly to get away from the group. The laughter encircled the group, long past Olivia's return to seat, this was mostly to do with the sour look on her face. Slowly however the laughter subsided, leaving a silence that was broken by Kimberley clearing her throat and continuing her story.

"A little-known fact that is held only by some of his closest friends, that Dorian is asexual. I don't this had always been the case however, it's my belief that after the war, both on foreign sole and home ground, that Dorian lost interest in finding a companion. With the stories that he has told me of what happened, I'm surprised he continues to socially function as well as he does. I think it's also the reason Lexa could be so honest with him, she is just as damaged as he is." The tone of the room shifted slightly for a slight second and Kimberley panicked about if she had said the wrong thing. She has never thought that Dorian or the others in the group were damaged, on the contrary, they were amongst the strongest people that she knew. Ben must have caught her thought in the air, because he smiled at her as he nodded his head and motioned slowly for her to continue, quietly, so the others wouldn't see. "So, what I asked him was less to do with that and more to do with his visits in general. They generally went the same way, with one or more of my friends were involved in that day's activity. So last night I finally asked him directly, if he was purposefully choosing activities that would involve my friends.

'I'm surprised it took you so long to noticed.' Dorian laughed. 'Your friends wanted to help, and I thought it was the best way to include them.' He went silent for a moment and continued in a softer tone 'I have a different plan for tonight... as you know, it is the anniversary of the Battle of Champions tonight, I would normally have asked Lexa come with me, but...'

'But considering she is off fighting overseas, you thought you'd ask me to come with you?' I finished and which he nodded in agreement.

We took his car to the event later that night, not a flashy thing at all. It was an old muscle car, black, with large scratches and dents. From what I could tell, they had been caused by Dorian using his power to pull the dents out, but that's all I know. Dorian did tell me all the specifications of it, but I didn't understand I word. But anyway, the event was being held in the Hall of Conflict, the refurbished church over on fifty-second street, it's got changed four or five years ago, I'm not quite sure. To pay tribute to fallen soldiers throughout our entire history. Each room is dedicated to a specific battle that changed the course of our country. The event for the Battle of Champions was being held in the very back room, as the rooms are structured chronologically from the main entrance and all connected by a central hallway. I was worried that I would be imposing on a traumatic event. I was only three years old when the battle had taken place. I got there however, I was greeted with smiles and friendly conversation. Literally, as I walked in, Dorian and I were separated and I was dragged to one side of the room and berated with stories, from what they did during the war to how well they were doing after, I think they were grateful for a fresh face. It took me over two hours to find Dorian again. He was standing in front of the large statue on the left-hand side of the room. I thought he would be admiring his own likeness in marble. As I got close enough however, I saw that it was not the statue of Dorian, which I later found on the other side of the room. It was that of his adversary, Godric Stormcrow. He was younger than

I thought he was going to be, only eighteen years old when he died, but he held himself high. He was clad in the elegant cloth of a Verthollow High commander, with a stream of medals over both sides of his shoulder with a cloak draped over his other shoulder. His posture was up and back, he had a small crow on perched on his outstretched right arm. Supposedly to gather Intel by sending the bird ahead, Dorian laughed when I read this off the inscription on the base.

Godric Stormcrow

Beloved son and war hero to the people of Verthollow. Who died with honour and secured peace between our two nations.

'I wouldn't believe that kid, it also says he was noble born, but that's a lie as well.' Dorian stated as he rested his hand on the base. 'He was a good man though, fearless, right until the end.'
'What did actually happen that day?' The words were out of my mouth before I had the chance to stop them. He didn't answer right away, he just stared up at the statue's face for a while longer.
'There's a lot of things that aren't common knowledge about the war, the Nekrüm's for example aren't profound healers doing the goddess's work. They act more like vultures on the battlefield, picking up the fallen, whether they be an ally or not. Enemies were actually preferred, they could exact intel out of them.' He turned and walked over to get a drink from the refreshment table, not even waiting for me to follow. 'A soldier can be brought back from death five times and each time, we come back less than what we were.' I didn't know what to say to that, you hear monstrous fables about the war, but to hear Dorian talk about it so casually, it was unnerving. I tried to console him by resting my hand on his forearm, but he moved it to take another sip of his drink. 'But Godric was different, I couldn't tell you if he was lucky or just naïve of the situation. The only time that I met him, he had no pain that I could see. It was in the middle of the Bethram sea, just south of the Verthollow Naval High command. Large super carriers from both sides plastered

the waters, each side had their weapons trained on the other, ready to fire. Neither side moved out of formation however, they couldn't. Waiting in the no man's land in between the two armies, sat a solitary ship. Smaller than the others and instead of weaponry there was a makeshift arena. It was agreed that the two 'champions...'.' Dorian scoffed at that title, '...would fight and the victor would decide which side was victorious. The way it's told in here, you'd think the fight went on for days, with neither side coming out on top for more than a moment.'

'That's not what happened?' I asked him and he tightly shook his head.

'No, the fight lasted for no more two minutes, if that. You see, Godric was very consumed by his own glory. When stepped into the arena, he started spatting off about who he was and how easy he was going to destroy me, playing up to the crowd, using all the titles he had been given.' Dorian drank the last of his drink and sat it back on the table. He turned and looked me dead in the eyes. 'As soon as he was ready to fight, I snapped him neck and walked off.'

'Just like that?'

'Just like that.' Dorian confirmed. 'Because heroes don't exist like people want them to, Godric's plan was most likely kill me and though that act of winning the war, gain equal treatment for his people back in Verthollow, you saw how they were treated. There's nothing nobler than to want an end to that.' He paused for a moment for me to nod in agreement, which I did. There was a lot worse treatment of the Drem over there. 'But myself, I just wanted to go home and rest, I had been in the army since before he was born. So, I did what had to be done.' He stated so calmly, it filled my mind with questions. How could he be so cold-blooded, and I thought that he continued in the army for a while after that, were just some of the questions. Out of all the questions, there was one that overpowered the others.

'Is that the lesson you wanted to instil into Lexa? That heroes don't exist? I wouldn't think you would have put her through all that training only for her to decide that she didn't want to follow in your footsteps. The amount of times Lexa came back beaten down, both physically and emotionally, was more than I could count. And she still refused to give up, no matter what I said. After everything that has happened between the three of us, do you honestly think that plan would have worked?' As I expected, I got no reaction from him, no anger or even disagreement. He just stared at me for a moment and then grabbed another drink. 'Partly.'" He finally put in after a while. 'I may have left the army after that fight, but I never stopped defending my country. The first few years I become a mediator between those leaving the army and re-joining civilian life. The number of soldiers, both Humankind and Drem, that had felt broken seemed endless. Over a third of the veterans commit suicide, the rest did what they could. Some joined the police, to continue to protect people. Some decided that faith was the right way to go and dove head first into that. After the attempted assassination of then leader Karl Stread however, I just took a step back on how I helped, not completely, but enough. As the old saying goes. When people expect your success, they'll only remember your failures.' I never thought I would ever heard him talk about that.'

"Who's Karl Stread?" David asked confused, seeing as this event had happened nine years before he was born. It was Thomas, who told him about who he was. After his attack by Sternberg, Thomas pushed himself into reading about history, politics, science, anything and everything he could find.

"Senator Karl Stread was a religious zealot, who used his rhetoric to push his agenda of the exile and eventual annihilation of all Drem from Steelhaven. With many people believing that it was us that started the war with our very existence, it didn't take much effort on his part for him to gain office."

"That's not entirely accurate" Michael put in, his first words of the night. "While the events leading up to the war are readily disputed, the fact remains that the unequal distribution of Drem between Steelhaven and Verthollow is what snowballed aggression between the two nations eventually leading to war."

"So, you're saying that if we didn't exist, then the war wouldn't have happened?" Thomas bellowed

"No, of course not, I just meant that you can't deny the negative effects Drem have. Having that amount of power, gives your kind natural advantages over…"

"Your kind!" David shouted, shooting up on to his chair. This fiery debate spread throughout the group, until everyone was shouting over each other. It was only Kimberley, who stayed quiet, resting her hands on her lap and staring at her open palms.

"You say that like we choose to have power, you have no moral ground to…" Ben abruptly stopped his conversation with Olivia when he saw Kimberley. He brushed past several of those in the group and knelt in front of her. Olivia followed, reciting her argument behind him. That was until she saw why he had stopped talking and instead sat next to Kimberley also, reaching out and holding her hand.

"I'm sorry, I never meant to cause this fight." Kimberley whispered, tears falling down her cheeks. Slowly the raised voices died down as they turned, one by one towards her.

Ben took to the floor and asked, "Do you want to continue with your story?" Trying to meet her gaze by lowering his head. Kimberley glanced at him for a second, then shook her head.

"It's okay if you don't want to." Heather stated as she sat on the other side of her. "We're here to talk about anything, you know that. Sometimes, we disagree but it's never any one person's fault."

"That's only because last argument you caused was worse, about whether the Omegans should be killed off or not." Gavin addressed, smiling as he did so. "I'm still saying no, just so you're aware." Heather stuck her tongue out at him, and the rest of the group laughed. "So, if we can forgive my girlfriend's genocidal thoughts, then your topic is nothing."

Kimberley smiled at that and nodded.

"Dorian had always been a firm believer on freedom of expression, not matter the intent behind their ideals. No one should be silenced for their opinion, no matter how many people agree with that belief. So, when senator Karl Stread was giving a public speech outside the registration building, on continuing dangers of unchecked Drem, a long-ranged sniper attempted to assassinate him. Dorian said that he was grateful that he was asked to protect the man. Because if he hadn't been on stage, he wouldn't have noticed the flash of light from the sniper's scope a second before the shoot was fired. After that, Drem all around the country and even some Humankind, began to condemn him as a traitor to his people. What they didn't understand was that he never agreed with any of the senators polices. There were many recorded instances of him actively deifying those ideals. One of his ideas involved another refurbishment of the church of Neitpose, the sea god. Where Humankind could better understand the nature of Drem and where Drem had communal place for better control of their abilities, so that they wouldn't pose a threat to anyone. The church itself was going to be moved to the Bethram sea, right in between the borders of Steelhaven and Verthollow. So that the institution would be completely neutral. The idea never truly got off the ground. Some even saw the plans for the relocation of the church to be another way to extradite Drem out of both countries and so furthering the divide between the two groups. This isn't what brought me in tonight however." Kimberley sighed softly and looked around the group for a moment, then down at floor.

"Dorian has been invited into joining the Nephilim." She finally revealed.

"What makes you think that?" Asked Ben, with others chiming in on the question.

"I apologised for the treatment he experienced simply for standing up for his morals, Dorian didn't seem concerned. I placed my drink down on the table and excused myself, claiming that I needed to find the bathroom, he saw through my ruse and asked me to look at something else instead. He was reached into the inside pocket of his suit and pulled out a small note.

> Dear Mr Dorian Black,
> Consider this an open invitation to have a conversation about your idea of the Power institute. Birerath, I believed you called it. We feel that it is truly a noble goal that shouldn't have been dismissed so easily.
> We have some very inflectional people in our group and with our help, we are sure that your dream come become a reality.
> We hope to hear back from you soon, Champion of Steelhaven.

'I found a street urchin phasing this letter through my front door a couple of months ago, he got away before I could question him however. Turn it over.' Dorian instructed, and I did so. On the back sat a shimmering light, it was faint, but noticeable. As I examined the letter, the light from above revealed the shape of a set of crystal wings. If he had shown anyone this letter before the church attack, no one would have given it a second thought. Since that night however, this symbol has been appearing more and more around the country. I'm sure you've noticed them. As soon as I saw the full emblem, I asked him what he was keeping this for.

'Why do you still have this? If anyone finds you with this, you could be in some serious trouble.' I think he understood for the most part, until he took the letter from me and placed it back into his jacket. We argued for a long time after that, about the implications of affiliating with this Drem extremist group. It was in that moment when Dorian's demeanor changed, became aggressive, it scared me." Kimberley's hand began to shake, making Ben and Heather's hands shake as well. "I've never seen him so full of anger, with every word he spoke, I could feel the loathing growing in him. It was still very subtle, if you didn't know him, you wouldn't have even known that it was there. I tried my best to change his mind, but he wasn't hearing any of it." Kimberley's hand tightened around the pair of hands holding them. "What if this was the reason that he never showed up to help at the church, or at the registration building. They had already gotten to him and convinced him not to intervene. Hell, he could have been persuaded months before that, I have no concrete evidence of when, or how he got this letter. It's just his word."

A deathly silence filled the room as the group began to understand what this all meant.

CHAPTER THREE

The door of Max's cell was pushed open by a pair of Omegan soldiers, dragging the beaten down husk of Grent inside. He wheezed heavily as his guards carried him through the doorway and dropped him onto the stone bed next to Max's who gave them a casual nod as they left. Grent convulsed in pain, lifting himself up, he looked over at Max. "I'm glad that my friend cares so much." He snapped, watching as Max continued to write his letter. He mumbled something in agreement but did not look up. "It's been three weeks, we've been moving from one shit hole to another. Why the fuck do you continue writing those letters?" Unlike Grent, how could barely stand, Max had little to no injuries that could be seen.

"It calms my nerves, that and I made a promise to my father that I would write to him once a week, no matter what." He replied as Grent staggered over to him, resting against the back of his chair. "I'm just explaining what's happened so far, for example, did you know that The Red Jackal has a Drem detection system over the main entrance? Means anyone with a power couldn't come in even if they wanted to."

"No shit." Grent replied as he pushed himself off Max's chair and moved back to his bed "Are you sure that this place is your true calling? You're clearly a master detective, maybe you should go join the police instead." Grent slowly lowered himself onto his bed, exhaling sharply as his back touched the cold surface.

"Would also mean I wouldn't have to look at your ugly mug again."

"You do know that I could just walk over there and beat you, right? It's not like you could put up much of a fight." Max questioned, not even bothering to look up from his letter.

"Would still be free of your face, I'd be okay with that." Grent responded as he lifted his arm to shield his eyes from the light above. Max laughed under his breath at that remark and continued to write. After a few moments, a guard appeared at their cell door. "...Oh, and that strategy you said I should adopt against that big bastard, Barron? Did not work." Grent told him, still covering his eyes. "I parried the first few of his attacks, but his sheer size overpowered me."

"Then you didn't do exactly as I said, Barron's size is his also his weakness, he over reaches and leaves himself vulnerable." Max replied as he finished his letter and rested back on his chair, stretching behind him. "So, I'm guessing you're out of the running for the next mission for our course, what is that fourteen months in a row now." Max mocked, causing Grent to throw his dinner bowl over to him, missing him by inches.

"You two, on your feet now!" The guard commanded. With a shift movement from Max, he had stood up and dragged Grent onto his feet. This sudden change coursed him to bark in pain. Max knew what would have happened if the guard had moved into their cell and them not ready for his instructions. As with the rest of the guards, he was covered from head to heel in pitch black metal plating with a detachable mask. This would normally cause the guard's voice to be muffled, a voice projector was installed into the mask however, nullifying this effect and causing all the guards to sound the same. The panic from Max was entirely unnecessary as the guard did not enter and instead directed them from the outside. "Conroy, get into your combat armour, it's time for your test." At that, the guard put his back to the door and waited.

"And what of mine? That bout was unfair!" Grent shouted at

him but got no reply. He rushed over and slammed his foot against the door, knocking himself onto the ground.

"Finally, because I'm tired of waiting." Max said quietly to himself as he moved over to the metal locker at the end of his bed, opening it up to reveal the full suite of body armour that was given to him on his first day of training. It was made of carbon-fibre-reinforced polymer that was almost completely covered in dried blood. It had originally been made for someone considerably larger than himself. That or it had been made too large as the other initiates had the same size armour and had to use the large straps around each piece, to tighten it to the body. This did not include the helm however, so many of them would go without one. This suited Max well as he felt a helm restricted his vision. Along with the armour was a wooden longsword and shield. Swordsmanship built character, at least that was the excuse his Omegan commanders had told Max. He knew better however.

"I'll tell you how well the mission goes when I get back." Max mocked as the guard opened their cell door.

"I'll see you in five minutes" Grent shouted after him.

As Max walked into the arena, the crowd rowed with applause, drowning out the announcer. The only thing that could be heard over the crowd was the two combatant's code names for the new Omegan mission, Hunter, which was Max's and Barron, whose real name was only known by a few. He was a well-built man who looked like he must have spent half of his life training. Unlike Max's armour, Barron stood without anything protecting his upper body. His loyalty to the Omegans was only matched to his hatred towards Max. Not only had he disgraced one of his idles on the same night he had been allowed to join, he had bested Barron in every fight since then, cheating him out of finding any more glory since then. His angry rushed through him so as soon as the large portcullis lowered behind him. Barron charged at full speed, holding his wooden bastard sword high above his head. Max flung the shield high in the air and rolled to his right out of the way. A fraction of a second later Barron's strike split the shield in two. Max ran to the other side of the cage and turned to face his adversary. Something was different about Barron, Max knew. He had a fury that hadn't been present in any other of their fights. His tactful mind had vanished, to be replaced with primal fury. It wasn't until Max saw him in the light could he see how he had been altered. Apart from the large, scarification tattoo of the Omegan symbol displayed proudly just above his heart. There were large, circular scorch marks over his torso. On both of his shoulders, his right pec and several running down both sides of his ribs. His eyes were full of hate. He rushed again, driving forward and thrusting his sword. Max narrowly dodged this attack but couldn't evade the back-handed strike that followed. Max was knocked onto his back, blood from his mouth spraying across the floor. Barron lifted his sword with his left hand and began to bring it down on to Max. He rolled out the way and gave Barron a back hand of his own as he passed. Rolling onto his feet, he struck Barron's left wrist with his own wooden longsword, breaking the wrist and causing him to drop his weapon. Max then drove his knee into Barron's jaw, slamming him flat on his back. The scream of applause from the crowd was deafening, but from the cries Max heard an all too familiar voice.

"Get up and kill him!" Darnall command silenced them all in an instant. The crowd stood frozen, looking over to the balcony were he and some of the other leaders sat. "I'm am tired of this boy thinking he can be one of us." Darnall raised his hand and pointed his finger at Max. "You do not belong here, now stop wasting time Barron and do as I command!" His words echoed around the room. It was then that Max realised that it was Darnall who had tortured Barron, had broken one of his most loyal soldiers all in the name of getting revenge.

Max lifted his sword horizontally in front of him and let it fall to the floor.

"Why call me to this fight?" Max shouted as he walked slowly over to the unconscious body of Barron. "Why even allow to join this fucking group in the first place if I can't do anything?" He didn't wait for a response, he knelt over Barron's body and began to punch him in rapid succession. Breaking his jaw, his collarbone, and his left arm. Blood matted his hands. "This is what I think of your champion!" He shouted, being dragged off Barron, Max clawed his way at the broken body in front of him, trying desperately to continue. It took four guards to drag him away and push him onto his knees. "I have done everything you asked, beaten everyone you have put up against me." Max pushed against the guards holding him so that he could get to his feet but failed. "Look at your champion, I deserve this mission!"

"You deserve nothing! Now get him out of my sight!" Darnall commanded, his temper matching Max's.

"I'm afraid not, General." An icy cold voice spoke from behind him, Darnall slowly turned to see Donna walking down the steps to meet him at the front of the balcony.

"Commander Shinecroft, no one told me that you were back from the visit of the cathedral of Deven'ra. I'm glad to see you are well."

"Spare me your false sentiment, what's this I hear about you not allowing our new champion his due." Donna stated, looking down at Darnell from two steps above him.

"Perhaps my lady has forgotten, this is not to declare anyone a champion, this is simply to find the best agent for the job. And I saw that this boy cheat."

"On what grounds?!" Max shouted, again, trying to stand but failing.

"Quiet boy, your betters are talking." Donna commanded down, turning back to Darnall. Her expression unchanged. "We both know that now is not the time to be selective, a titan has joined their ranks. Just finish this already." 'Finally, someone here that was on my side,' Max thought to himself. "So give him the mission brief, so that we can focus on more important things."

"I suppose that's good enough." Max whispered as he was dragged back to his cell.

It was the next day, when Max found out on his mission. After the mission briefing, he was reconsidering his role in that plan. Recent intelligence from the merchant district, that all the Drem working in a shop called Smith and Taylor, barring the owner, had vanished overnight. The news of the previous owner, and father to the current was the starting point to Max's uneasiness about the whole thing. The implication is that the residents have been convinced into joining the ranks of the Nephilim. There was no concrete proof on this however, as the 'intelligence' was in fact just rumours gathered by supporters in the area, mostly comprising of the homeless. Apparently, this was how the Omegans gather intelligence, which was never what Max thought how the group found information. A homeless person, especially a Drem, would say anything for some money. Not only is it not reliable, Max thought, but was far from honourable. This impression was compounded when he had to talk to over a dozen different homeless to confirm their stories and deliver each of their rewards. Most of the stories were contradictory, some saying only the Drem were in hiding because of Max's friends attack on the shop. Others, saying that a Drem veteran from the war put them in hiding. Only a few even mentioned the Nephilim, and only in passing. Whenever Max told his commanding officer, he was shot down with the same rhetoric. 'Just do as you're told, I never wanted you on this mission in the first place.' Kaisar would say. Max didn't know any other members of the group, only by their code names. Kaisar oversaw the operation, he was a short man with an even shorter temper. He had commanded over a dozen operations, from thief of specialised items to the elimination of potential hostiles. This meant he had little patience for the constant stream of new recruits. His second in command, Duchess, was a lot calmer and worked as an intermediary between each squad member. With little experience in her role, Kaisar did not trust her. Tank stood as the squad's specialist. He was the only one of the squad that Kaisar trusted, as the pair were the only original squad members left. The rest of the squad had joined not long before Max, but he hadn't met them yet. He only knew their names, Vision and pyro. Vision was the other scout in the team and spent much of his time out in the field. Pyro has a hyperactive demolition expert, Max had heard. The team was all covered in the same uniform as Omegan initiates, except brand new and reinforced with additional padding. The faces of the group were all covered, including Max's, with a balaclava. The second phase of the operation was the reason why Max was hesitating about his role, He was set to interrogate a captured prisoner.

The room was dark, lit by a dim, blue light that swang overhead. It was pushed gently in all directions by of the wall vents that littered the ceiling. In the centre of the room sat the young prisoner in a chair, their upper body held up by chains wrapped around their forearms, linked to a steel pole overhead that itself was linked to the high ceiling. Their head was hung back as though they were unconscious. They had already gone through several rounds of 'treatment' already. A large bruise across the left side of the prisoner's face and a hint of another across their collarbone. Max looked down at the prisoner, pride gleaming through his mask, glad to see a Drem in their place. Regardless of the Drem's age, which he guessed was around ten years old. He walked forward slowly, stopping right in front of the prisoner. Concern rushed through him, 'maybe the prisoner was too injured for his questions' he thought. He reached out and pressed on the prisoner's side. The bawl of pain blasted out of them. "I haven't got much time to stand and talk, tell me what you know." Max instructed calmly, looking down at the boy and still holding his side. A fair few moments passed before Max released the pressure on the prisoner's ribs, causing his prisoner to cough sharply.

"Malik Taylor, owner of the Smith and Taylor and I have no idea where my employees are." He recited coldly as though he had repeated that same answer all day, looking down at the floor and away Max's gaze. He replied to this by reapplying the pressure on the prisoner's ribs, with a soft crunch as his two fingers pushed further in. The prisoner's cried loudly, bringing cheers from the outside.

"That's not what I asked, now we know that you had a visit from a young woman in the early hours of the yesterday morning, with several of your employees leaving with her." Max released Malik's ribs again. The boy panting heavily and twisted his torso to protect himself. Max put pressure onto Malik's shoulder. "Dark hair, light grey hoodie and jeans. They were last seen over at the Dreadbourne district, where they vanished. Now where were they going?"

"I don't know, I don't know where they went after they left my shop." Malik pushed out between breaths. Max stood over him, calm and still. He bent down and looked the prisoner in the eyes. 'Perhaps I have pushed him to far,' Max thought. 'It's not his fault that this boy was born with…I'm not even sure what his ability is.'

"And why do I find that hard to believe?" Max inquired as he grasped Malik firmly around the throat and standing up, lifting the boy off his seat. "You were there when they had the meeting, you must have heard what was said." Max continued to pull Malik up with every statement, lifting him off the floor and against the chains holding him to the ground. The shackles rubbing Malik's ankles raw. "Do you honestly expect me to believe that you heard nothing about what was happening and where they were going?" Max's grip around the prisoner's throat lifted his face up to the light and constricted his windpipe. Gasping for air, he tried his best to answer. But there was no use, he blacked out. As soon as he did, the worry Max had felt vanished and hatred began to creep its way back in. It was at this moment that Max finally realised that the boy had been using his power. It was also when Pyro, decided to walk in and see if

Max had my any progress.

"Hey, hey, hey, did you get any more information out of this kid? Kaisar is having a small meltdown about it taking too long." Pyro spat out as she walked through the door, not reacting to Max's anger. She walked over next to him and looked over their prisoner. "Aww, did the poor baba fall asleep?" She reached into the bag on her thigh and pulled out a flare. "I could burn a hole into his sternum, maybe that keep him awake. At least he'll be able to breathe."

"Maybe, but we can't get the info we need if he's too busy dying." Max replied, still staring at Malik.

"This is true, oh well" Pyro sighed, lowering the flare to her side.

"Maybe after though, this fucker thought it was acceptable to use his power on me."

Pyro laughed at that, which drew Max's glare. "Yeah, Kaisar wanted to know how the emotion manipulation worked on someone who didn't know it was going on. It was really funny." Pyro bust out laughing at that, still staring at Malik's unconscious body. In frustration, Max smashed the prisoner's undamaged ribs, he then slammed the boy back into his seat which caused him to wake up gasping for air.

"Try that again, and I won't stop, now talk!" Max commanded, all the anxiety he had felt before had not returned. He stared coldly at the boy and was about to hit him again when Malik began to respond. He took a collection of short breaths and looked up at his abductors, swaying uneasily he spoke one solitary name.

"Darek Cowan."

Vision took over the assignment of finding this target, as he had been watching from the surveillance cameras, he had secretly placed all around the squad's makeshift base. He spent most of his time out in the city. So much so, that only Kaisar and Duchess knew what he looked like. He had been a transferred from another group about a week before Max joined. He had only meet the two leaders for a short briefing before leaving to gather information. He had been the same in his last group and several others before that. This habit became his speciality as he knew the streets of Steelhaven better than anyone else. This also meant that within the hour, Vision had relayed the location of his target to Tank, who 'convinced' his target to come with him. The full extent of how he did this wasn't apparent until Tank sauntered through the secret entrance to the base, with his target slung over his shoulder. Kaisar wished to find out the exact details of that night for himself, or that's what Max got told as he was commanded to collect supplies from a nearby outpost. This frustrated Max, yet another time when he was being left behind while important things were happening. As with other times however, he took several deep breaths and did his duty. The outpost sat in the Snowwynne district, in a neighbourhood overshadowed by the Alopia mountain which housed the central government building. A giant castle constructed out of the peak of the very mountain itself. Over a dozen towers protruded tall like thorns, with only a small portion of ramparts connecting them. Each tower governed a specific part of government. On top of each high point spiked conical roofs made of Talgane. As the mountain descended, four outer walls stood to protect the main base, each standing taller than the first but all levelling off at the top. The last of the outer walls housed the military base. Made entirely of Talgane and half the size of the final wall, with the square defences falling to ground level. Two watchtowers on the corners. All the government officials and military personal were housed under all of this. As Max walked through the empty streets, rechecking the list of supplies required. He looked back down to find himself walking through a graveyard. The silence, coupled with the shadow of the mountain, filled him with distrust of the place. As he walked through, he felt a sense of familiarity to the place however, which was odd, he hadn't stepped much farther out of Ulton all his life. It was also one of the many reasons why he stayed in the Omegans in the first place, to see more of the country. Walking down the main path of the cemetery, rows of gravestone lined on either side, Max noticed a figure to his left. He walked passed as quietly as he could, trying not to disturb them.

"Hello?" A soft voice questioned him from behind, causing him to stop in his tracks. "Sorry, I didn't realise anyone else was here. Are you here to visit anyone? I... well it's complicated." The voice continued, moving closer to Max, he slowly turned around to see a young woman. She had long, curly hair pulled back and held by a black, silk scarf. She was wearing a full-length silk black dress, with a purple corset, lining and gloves. She had a kind face and some reason that Max couldn't explain, he felt calmed by her presence. He smiled slightly before shaking it off and replying to her.

"Yes, I mean no, sorry..." Max blustered before clearing his throat. "I was just passing through, I didn't mean to disturb you." He reached out a hand. "I'm sorry for your loss." He smiled to her sympathetically.

"Don't worry about it, I'm here on behalf on someone. My... friend, she, she couldn't be here today, she's away. It didn't seem right for her parents to be alone on this day." The woman stammered through her words, Max could see the pain and tried to console her but finding difficult to think of the best way.

"My name is Maxwell Conroy." He was surprised by his own honesty, something he couldn't explain. But he didn't shy away from it, their hands shook firmly.

"Kimberley Sangster" the woman replied. This also caused Max to smile gleefully.

"I knew I'd seen you somewhere, I'm a huge fan. Especially with your new work, can I ask what inspired you to write..." Max began to ask before he realised where he was, he hung his head while Kimberley laughed.

"Don't worry, it's fine." She smiled, feeling more relaxed now.

Dozens of questions swam through Max's head, from where Kimberley saw her career would go in the next few years to how she found Verthollow and if she would visit other countries. All these questions disappeared when he remembered his current mission and realised there wasn't time.

"I'm sorry Miss Sangster…" he started, standing back up right.

"Kimberley please" She replied kindly

"Kimberley…" Max corrected himself uncertainly. "I have so many questions, but I'm afraid I need to be…somewhere, so I don't have time to ask them. Sorry." Max looks down in shame.

"That's okay," Kimberley reassured, meeting his gaze. Max couldn't help but be happy about that, and again he couldn't explain why. Kimberley reached into the handbag draped over her left forearm and pulled out a small card. "Call this number, that's my agent. He can arrange a meeting for us for you to ask any questions you want." It was then that Kimberley reached out her own hand and shook Max's. He smiled broadly at this, thanked her as calmly as he could. He then pulled his hand away and gave her a small wave before awkwardly turning around and continuing on with his mission.

CHAPTER FOUR

The fear that Kimberley felt fractured her to her core, the cloth hood over her head, thick and unyielding, keeping her feeling weary. All she could do was focus on her breathing. Whomever was holding her captive was Drem, that she knew for certain. The power dragging her along was telekinetic, soft like water and yet hard like stone. Any movement that she made, consciously or not, was countered, keeping her frozen. All around her, silence followed. Only the footsteps of her guard outside could her heard. She counted the guard's footsteps, trying to gauge how far away they were from her. The last thing she remembered, she was walking up to her home after coming back from visiting Lexa's parents graves. Lucas and Helen O'hearn, who had died a three years ago, the specifics were difficult to procure. Lexa's grief was understandably overwhelming, so she did not ask her. Instead Kimberley asked the police involved, the only thing they would say was that there had been a car accident on a remote country road. So, on the anniversary of her parent's marriage, she and Lexa would visit their grave to leave flowers. After joining the army however, Lexa could not do her part, so that responsibility fell to Kimberley. 'The first time she visits by herself and this happens,' Kimberley thought, not immune to the irony. Her guard had a stagger to his walk, pausing from time to time. Kimberley concluded that this was a change in direction, however, this happened so frequently that she lost both her count and any sense of direction. A pressure across her chest sprang harshly on her, slowing her breathing and causing her to lose conscious.

When she woke up, Kimberley found herself sprawled across a concrete floor. The metallic blue of the floor spread to the entire room with a bright light from above. She raised her eyes up to the source to be met with large glowing orbs of white light. They encircled with other, lifting and falling around the entire ceiling. Kimberley reached out slowly to lift herself up. As soon as she did, a force from above compressed her hard to the ground, causing the air in her lungs to disappear. Her bones began to crack from the weight, but she would not give them the satisfaction of hearing her scream. She instead buried her face into the ground as a sign of submission and prayed they would relent. The force holding her down melting through her and across the floor. Kimberley gasped harshly for breath but remained motionless. Watching the ground, Kimberley stare was interrupted when the lights above flickered, slowly at first but steadily increased. The lights pulsated above her, forcing Kimberley to close her eyes.

"Stand!" A command echoed around the room, a collection of voices commanded, separated between repetitions, the loudest of them must have been the leader, Kimberley thought. Whomever had walked in did not wait for Kimberley to comply, she was pulled up against her will and into the air. The energy that held her began to push her limbs apart, with her head lifted high, pressing the base of her skull into her neck. On reaction, Kimberley shut her eyes. Perhaps if she didn't look at them, it would keep her alive. That idea was pushed aside when her captures pulled open her eyes, forcing her to watch. The figure in front of Kimberley stood smothered in shadow, which sprayed around their body. Their appearance changed with a flourish of said shadow. Spinning slowly up and around their body in several figures of eight, one layer on top of another. As the shadow reached the being's head, it descended violently down in front of them. At first there stood a man covered in muscles, tall and imposing. Then a small girl, who's shadow sparked with colour. The girl lifted her hand and from it was projected a transparent image of the man Kimberley had meet earlier that day, Maxwell. The being then shifted to that of a slightly older girl, teenager perhaps, with sparks of blue lightning washed through her. "Do you know where this man is hiding? We know you meet him in a graveyard, there would be no reason to meet a stranger there. Telling us that you two in fact knew each other and are working together." The collection asked, repeating their statement after each other. Although each individual voice overlapped the next, Kimberley could distinguish between them. She did not say a word however, her fear kept her from replying. Max's image vanished as the collection stepped forward. "Or do you expect us to believe your relationship between a known Omegan soldier doesn't exist? You had been in relationship with a Drem for over fifteen years. And yet, you turn your back on that." The collection inquired, shifting into another form, that of a teenage boy whose hands held shining bright crystals. This appearance seemed more solid than the others, as the encircling shadow slowed around him. Kimberley was shifted down to meet the collection's eyes. She tried to push away from them as she noticed the shadow began to leech itself onto her. The force holding her up noticed this and pushed Kimberley closer. The shadow creped slowly up Kimberley's body, terror washed through her as the shadow moved up her neck. Her surroundings began to shake violently with bright light shining behind the collection. They noticed this and shifted back towards the light, facing Kimberley one moment and instantly facing the light the next as the shadow washed over them. The back of the collections head fractured to white through cracks in its skin as it screeched in fury. The collection rushed back through to face towards, their form shifting frantically through their looks as they reached over and grabbed at Kimberley. "You have no right to take this from us!" The collective demanded to the room, the light slowly enveloping everything. The shadow began to pull back from Kimberley and spread back behind the collection to combat the light advancing towards them. Suddenly, the light shoot took control of the room in an instant, washing away what Kimberley could see.

Kimberley's vision returned slowly to the room to see the last person she was expecting, Dorian. He was kneeling in front of her and offering his hand to help her up. Instead, she moved away and pushed herself up, using the wall behind her to steady herself. "What, what are you doing here? What am I doing here? What the hell is this place?" She questioned, shaking slightly as she found it difficult to stay on her feet. She lifted her hand to signal Dorian to move away as he moved forward to help. "No, not until you answer my questions." Kimberley crocks out through her fear.

"I understand your hesitant to trust this current situation…" Dorian begins but is interrupted

"So, answer my questions!" Kimberley shouted, her fear rushing passed her. Dorian stood up and stepped back out of respect.

"This is a place I didn't wish you to see, it's a place of the Nephilim. Or more precisely, a Nephilim training facility. From what I gather they have dozens of places like this around the city. With more being creating every month. But this isn't about that." Dorian moved close to Kimberley and whispered down her ear. "They are looking for Lexa and they believe you know where she is."

"Lexa? The image they showed me wasn't Lexa but some guy I had just meet. Either way, why didn't they just ask you? You seem to have aligned yourself with them." Kimberly whispered back in a revolted tone. Since they announced themselves, the Nephilim have attacked both Humankind and Drem. Hundreds of people have been wounded or killed. 'Why should I trust anything that he has to say?' Kimberley though, looking at him with revulsion. Dorian cold stare would have normally made Kimberley falter, she had now lost all respect for him. Dorian took a deep breath in and reached into his inner coat pocket, pulling out a small black box. "What's that you have there?" Kimberley asked coldly.

"I never thought I'd be the one to do this, the plan was for her to awaken your memories after her investigation was all over. Life, it seems, continues to be unkind." Dorian reached out and tried to pass the box over, but Kimberley didn't move. "Please, this is very important." Dorian asked, concern filling his gaze. Despite her better judgement, Kimberley snatched the box off him and held it in both hands. She recognised it now was closer. She slowly opened it to reveal a beaded necklace with an onyx medallion shaped in a three-headed falcon held in the centre.

"Where did you get this? The last time I saw this, it was around Lexa's neck as she left for basic training. She hadn't taken it off since I had given it to her. I don't understand." Kimberly asked but got no reply. It was only when she touched the necklace, was everything made clear.

She was back in the hospital room with Lexa, back to the night that she wished had never happened. This time however, something was different. Lexa looked kindly at her as she held Kimberley's hand with both if hers. "I have to go undercover in the Omegans, the higher ups believe that The Nephilim have an influence over them, so they can sow discourse to gain a foothold in Steelhaven. They also believe, and I agree, that my power would be a great asset in bringing a peaceful end to it all quicker." Lexa instructed. "My priority is to keep you safe and to do that, I need to change."

"What do you mean? Change your memories?" Kimberley responded, tightening her grip of Lexa's hands.

"That and physically, for the best results I need to change into a new person. I choice Maxwell Conroy..."

"Wasn't he your first, your only boy crush?" Kimberley replied, smirking. Lexa sighed and nodded at this.

"He is going to be based largely on Dorian in fact, a hero beyond fault." Lexa jested, kissing Kimberley's hand. "This also means I need to change your memories…"

"…If you're sure, what do you need me to do?" Kimberley asked hesitantly. Lexa smiled warmly at her girlfriend.

"Always ready to dive in head first sweetie?" Lexa asked playfully. Receiving a nod back. "This will mean that you'll think we have broken up, are you alright with that?"

Kimberley twists their hands over and kisses Lexa's right hand. "If it needs to be done sweetheart, then it needs to be done. I trust you."

Before Kimberley could recite any information that the necklace revealed, Dorian covered her mouth with his left hand. "I need you to remember this, you need to understand why you're protecting this man." Dorian flinched slightly and stepped back. "I'm sorry that I can't do more to help. Just remember, if you get overwhelmed, just call for me." Before Kimberley could ask what, he meant, Dorian had vanished, leaving her alone in her prison.

PART THREE

CHAPTER ONE

Malik had never been out of the market district in his life. In fact, apart from arranging deliveries of raw material, Malik didn't communicate much with the outside world. So, finding Mr Black's house was difficult. As a war veteran, most of his records were sealed off from the public. It was only when he met with the Merchant Guild, comprising of some of the oldest and most powerful families in the country, did he have any notion of where his house was. The meeting had been planned since he had taken over his father's estate. So, they could oversee the changeover in power, while Malik could network his way through and gain a stronger client base for the shop. After the night just gone however, he did not care about any of that. Only about getting his family back and what they rest of the guild had planned. Very little, or at least something that they didn't wish to include him in. This led to his secondary plan of the night, to confront Mr Black. The moment he closed his shop, Malik rushed over to Mr Black's home, full of fury. It was only when Malik found himself standing in front of his door and after he had already knocked, did Malik feel a sudden rush of panic. He wanted to run but was frozen to the spot. 'Should I confront him about this? I don't want it to happen like last time.' Malik asked himself, waiting for the door to open. Ideas of how to stop this confrontation went through Malik's head, perhaps he could hold the door closed was one of the many that he was considering. As he reached forward to put his plan into action, the door swung inwards to reveal Mr Black towering over him. All the blood rushed out of Malik's face as he stared up unable to speak. His stony glare did not help Malik's nerves to ease and after a couple of minutes of silence, Mr Black stepped back and shut the door in Malik's face. He turned and began to rush down the road, back to safety. Just as he was about to turn the corner, he stopped himself, "No, I need to know!" he berated himself, striding back to the door and knocked louder than before. He tried to take in slow deep breaths but only could find short, shallow ones. Unlike before, the door swung open to reveal Mr Black's home.

"If you're going to come in, do it quickly. I'm trying to keep the heat in." A voice projected out from behind the door. On gut reaction, Malik rushed in. It was only when he was inside, did the heat of Mr Black's home flow over him. It was sudden and overwhelming, opposite to the downpour outside. The raindrops that had fallen over him began to float off and into the air, collection in a ball above his head. On trying to turn and close the door, Malik realised that he himself was floating a foot off the floor since he walked inside. "I'm assuming you like lamb, correct?" Mr Black asked as he pushed the collected water out and closed the door.

"Y-yes Sir." Malik replied, full of nerves and confusion, had someone notified Mr Black of his visit.

"Good." Mr Black boomed out from the kitchen. Malik felt the hold of Mr Black's power as he pulled the boy forward and sat him down at the oak dining table adjacent to the kitchen. Malik began to shake on the table out of nerves, so to calm down Malik stared down at the table, not wanting to ware out stay his welcome before he could get through the reason as to why he was there.

"Were you expecting someone? I-I hope I haven't intruded." Malik asked quietly.

"No, but after my inadequate support at the shop the other day. I knew it was only a matter of time before you would show up wanting answers." Mr Black responded as he walked through from the kitchen with two lamb dinners hovering behind him. Malik noticed that one disk was significantly smaller than the other leading him to believe it had been made from a portion of Mr Black's dinner, this made Malik feel a spark of guilt. "Correct?" He asked moving his chair out and sitting down, Malik nodded as his meal was placed in front of him. "I'm assuming the first thing you want to know is why I didn't do more the help you deter the four of your employees from leaving with that woman...Kate, correct?" Again, all Malik could do was nod, lifting his head slightly to meet Mr Black's gaze and so not to seem rude. "All I could do was give them my opinion, it was ultimately their choice on whether they wanted to stay or go. Also, that legal assistant was doing more the push them into the deal than the recruiter was."

"Darek Cowan..." Malik whispered, barely audible

"I'm sorry, what was that?" Mr Black challenged.

"His name is Darek Cowan." Malik repeated nervously "He works over at B-B-Bashert Solicitors, the legal office over on the edges of the financial district. He works f-for my f-f-father, he's been trying to get back my shop since his imprisoned." Malik pushed himself through his stammer the best that he could.

"Yes, I hear what you did as well." Mr Black pointed his knife over at Malik accusatory, which caused Malik to flinch.

"I'm-I'm not sure what you mean Mr Black." Malik responded under his breath, holding his shaking hands tightly together under the table so not to be noticed.

"Dorian, please." Mr Black replied, going back to his meal.

"Dorian." The name fell uncomfortably off Malik's tongue, causing him to stammer to worsen. "I did-didn't do a... anything, I swear."

"No, one of our mutual friend did though." Dorian looked up. "At any rate, you had the deed to the shop, by all legal rights you owned the business. Why didn't you ask him to leave?" Malik looked away at this, his reason was childish, he knew. 'What would happen if my father heard of me evicting one of his associates, for any reason. What kind of damage would he cause to my shop, let alone my reputation.' Malik thought but did not voice. After a short stillness between the pair Dorian sighed.

"Fear can make even the bravest person falter, it's only natural. But protecting your employees, whom I heard you think of as family; should take priority over a concern for a powerless man, both metaphorically and literally." Dorian lowered down his cutlery with his mind as he looked over at the boy. "You're a smart kid, smarter than to allow anyone to be treated like this." Before Malik could answer, Dorian continued. "I am talking about this, you came here to confront me about what you see as an injustice. Yet you sit there, small and frail and not showing your anger. Maybe your power limits how much of your emotions you can show, although I doubt it." Dorian folded his arms as he straightened his back. "Take a moment and tell me how you saw it." Malik did just that and the nerves seemed to melt away, this was mostly to do with him using power inwardly. As he opened his eyes, he shifted his weight in his seat to match Dorian's seating position and began.

"It was a day that dragged more than most. Since I had gotten full ownership of Smith and Taylor, there had been less and less people visiting my business. Around a dozen customers had entered that day, with only three inquired about our services. With so little traffic into the building, the employee roster had slowly become more fluid. With the three on shift being changed every two hours to keep boredom low. It was in the last few hours of the day's shift when you walked in to talk to me."

"Yes, I remember, I came to tell you about Lexa's decision to join the military." Dorian interjected, allowing Malik to have a few bites of his meal.

"It was only when you were leaving my office, did we notice Kate and Mr Cowan. I'm not entirely sure if they had arrived together, she was talking to Chloe, the supervisor of that shift. While Mr Cowan was looking at the suits of show. I assumed he was just looking for yet another suit to add to the ones he had already acquired, I focused all my attention on Kate. She wore an exquisitely fitted dark blue cotton suit, with a similar gabardine overcoat and... sorry, force of habit." Malik stopped himself as he saw Dorian's eyes glazing over. "She looked nice, I'll leave it at that. Anyway, she had been there enough time to gain a rapport with Darren, Sara, Matt and Chloe. Chloe had previously worked over at Aine's Attire as a personal shopper, that was until she lost her job and had to go to the registration building to find another job."

"I'm assuming she was there when the Omegan attack happened, correct?" Dorian asked.

"Yes, we started talking after the event and I could see how terrified she was to go back into the building again. So, I gave her a job within my business instead. As soon as she saw us, she signalled me to come over. Kate turned to us and introduced herself to you first and then to myself, which I saw as odd. Anyway..." Malik continued passed Dorian's attempted objection. "In the time she had been in the shop, she had already convinced Darren and Sara to join. Darren had always been hesitant in staying at the shop at any rate, I think he stayed because of the same reason the others did. If they left, they would have to go be arrested for the conscious departure of a suitable profession. Kate's rhetoric was highly religious from what I heard, it made me feel very uncomfortable."

"Is that because you don't believe in Deven'ra?" Dorian questioned

"No, I do." Malik assured, placing his own cutlery down. "The week following my father's arrest, there was a lot of reporters trying to find out everything they could about my family and myself; some wouldn't say a word. There were others however, who told them everything. From the frequency of the beatings, to what got them through the traumatic time. Religion; many of my brothers and sisters had copies of the Holy Shaddai which they read daily. It seemed to me that the recruiter was feeding off their most closely held beliefs to attract them over to her side." While Dorian did not reject this theory, he also didn't seem to accept it either. He just stared across the table. "After hearing that she had friends who could them find a better standing in life, would even be able to continue working here. Just not have to live in the same place that holds so many traumatic memories. Then you chimed in agreeing with her."

"It does seem strange that you would stay in that place, granted I know you wanted to keep the family business going. But why not moving the shop to a different spot. If I remember right, there is a building closer to the fountain. It would get you more business." Dorian countered, finishing his meal and placing the plate in the middle edge of the table, in parallel to the kitchen door.

"Because my family has owned that spot for over two hundred years, I'm not going to abandon it now. Besides, I have used a fair amount of my father's fortune to renovate the sleeping quarters under the shop." Malik was getting frustrated at this point, he collected his own empty plate up, went to stand up to place his plate with the other one. But instead Dorian moved them across for him. "A lifetime of pain should not darken my family's legacy." Even before he had finished, Malik knew he was wrong. "From the information that I could gather, from my meeting with the Merchant's guild…" He continued before Dorian could correct him. "Kate was a recruiter for the Nephilim, their symbols have been appearing all over the market district and I've heard of them popping up in other districts as well. I didn't notice it before but, she had the mark etched into the business cards she left us all." Malik pulled out a small card from his trouser pocket, it had all the recruiter's contact information. "While the information is fake or old, the symbol on the back is not." With a flick of his wrist, Malik threw the card over for Dorian to inspect. It flew high into the air causing Malik to be concerned that it wouldn't reach him. As it began to fall to the table Dorian caught the sheet of card swooped across the table and hovered in front of Dorian's eyes. The change was subtle at first, Malik wouldn't have even noticed if not for his ability. An upsurge of surprise rushed through Dorian. 'Perhaps he did not know about that.' Malik thought to himself, that was a step in the right direction. If he could bring Dorian to his side, then he could find them faster. "Do you have any information about them Mr… Dorian?" Malik asked, not wanting to lose his momentum. He just sat there staring, concerned that maybe he had not heard him. "I know little about their operations, only that they are a fundamentalist group, focused on bringing our kind to their 'rightful place' whatever that means. That information was confirmed by the Merchant Guild this morning, who have also lost several of their employees to this and I think that…"

"I will look into this, you have my word." Dorian commanded over the table in a finalising tone, shutting Malik off and causing him to shrink back into his chair again. The card was slowly lowered to the table so the pair could look at each other. Malik was concerned about if he had pushed too much, it was very difficult to measure what Mr Black was thinking. His eyes had grown cold as his emotions, what Malik could feel from him, had felt off far in the distance.

"I had a conversation with Mr Cowan also…" Malik continued, trying to keep a hold of his confidence. "And he said, while he wasn't actively there to cause any trouble. He was grateful that he was though." He stopped there, not wanting to sound condescending. 'We were both there' he thought, 'should I continue with my story.' This pause however, had attracted Mr Black's frustration, so Malik continued. "…With everything that Mr Cowan said, emphasizing how badly I handled the condition under my father's rule. He did with such vigour that it had drawn the rest of my brothers and sisters. From what I could tell, that wasn't a part of that recruiter's plan."

"What makes you say that?" Dorian wondered

"The slight absence of that way of speaking when the other children came up and joined us. I think he intention was a quick walk in, recruitment of a small group and then to move on to another business."

"It may explain why only the four from the original group went with her." Dorian interjected, to which Malik agreed. "So, what are your intentions from here? Or haven't you got much farther in terms of planning after this encounter?" Dorian asked, indicating to them.

"Right now, I just want answers as to why you didn't do more to help, while you didn't know about the woman's affiliations to the Nephilim. She and that rat were taking away my family. As a friend, I thought you would do more than you did." Malik's anger flushed for a moment as he stood. This did not seem to faze Dorian.

"As I promised, I will look into that woman's connections to this terrorist group, for lack of a better label. I will find out what their intentions are and get your family out of any undue…"

"When do we start?" Malik commanded with a strength he had not felt before. Dorian smiled and suggested for Malik to sit down but he did not.

"Soon."

CHAPTER TWO

No matter how Olivia's meetings with the other survivors went, she never slept that same night, this was mostly due to the nightmares she would have. Her first meeting with them brought forth the most vivid of those nightmare, a retelling of her assault. She told herself that it was because that meeting had been all about each member's experience. After several meetings went by and the same dream happened, whether Sternberg was even mentioned or not, she decided it was best not to sleep the night of the meeting. For the most part it worked, with the nightmares appearing few and far between. When she got back to her home in the far western side of the Dreadbourne district, Olivia walked quickly through her hallway and into the kitchen, it was a small room with oversized cabinets plastering the parallel walls, they were made of cheap plywood and covered in even cheaper white paint. She had started painting the room a bright colour in hopes to give the illusion of size. This had four months ago, and Olivia had only finished the second coat on three of the cabinets in the corner. In that corner sat Olivia's lifeblood, coffee. She made a strong mug with the intension on having several throughout the night. It was only when she entered the living room, her plans change. Just like the rest of her cramped home, the living room had enough room for the essentials, a two-seater sofa, a flat screen television on top of a wooden cabinet and a few family photos. The walls were a bleak shade of grey that in the midday sun would shine white. A sharp noise from outside drew Olivia's attention, a car alarm. She also saw something new. Sitting against her flat screen television was a small, folded piece of paper. Upon opening the note, Olivia regretted doing so instantly.

Liv,
I need your help over at the dojo
It's important.
Your father

She dropped the note onto the floor, gulps as much coffee that she could in one mouthful, burning her tongue slightly; with a small sigh, she grabbed her keys and dashed back outside and followed her summons.

It didn't take long for Olivia to arrive at her father's establishment, formally a church dedicated to an unknown god, as the statues had been either removed or destroyed. Olivia's father, Frank, brought the building off the church dirt cheap and refurbished it into a fighting dojo for the neighbourhood. There was no set style of fighting especially for either Humankind or Drem, as their specific power would indicate which form they would require. The Humankind would focus mostly on kick boxing or just boxing on its own, feeling more 'grounded' in those styles. The building itself was made of rock brought up from the ground, as were all the old buildings of Steelhaven. Two giant towers encased the wooden door on top of a flight of stairs. Just above the entrance stood a demolished statue, the head had gone and the rest of it gave no indication as to whom it was honouring. Even though it had none, Olivia still felt the statue's eyes glare down at her as she walked up to enter. Walking in, Olivia was welcomed by a familiar face, Faye. He was resting both his elbows on the wooden podium in front of him, his hand clasped together, resting his forehead on them with his eyes closed. The cold breeze from outside woke him up, bringing his gaze firmly onto Olivia. His eyes shown a bright shade of gold and had a firmness to them that could not be denied. Thick dreadlocks ornamented with wooden beads flowed down his back, that coupled with his muscular form was a definite sign to Olivia that her father had chosen the right bouncer. Although, Olivia knew the real why he got gotten the job. Faye Green was a rarity among the Drem, he was empathic, more specially Faye could read and understand a person's intentions. This had caused a problem between the pair the first time they meet. It had been a month since Sternberg's attack. Her father, not knowing of the assault, had all but given up on making her leave her home. As he saw it, his daughter had become lazy and he had spent too much of his valuable time trying to change that. It was only because of the support of the other victims; did Olivia pluck up enough courage to come and confess what had happened. Moments before doing so however, she decided against it and just let him think whatever he wanted, he did not need to know. Or she did not wish to tell him, he had a temper that Olivia had not seen, but heard the rumours surrounding it. She still walked into the dojo with a confidence, smiled politely at the new door man and walked to open the entrance to the upstairs office. It was then that Faye confronted her, his imposing presents scared her, he told, no demanded that she told her father the truth. Olivia shifted back from him, but he just grasped her forearm and pulled her towards him. Telling her how disrespectful she was being to her father and that he had a right to know, which made Olivia cower on the spot. Her confidence had been taken from her, it had been an effort for her to even reach the place for her to speak to her father again without bursting into tears. The times she had called him to tell him everything, only for her to hang up and chastise herself for not being strong enough, was more than she wanted to remember. It was only when Faye had threatened that he would go up and tell him instead did Olivia find her courage. It was not his secret to tell, she hit him with such force that he was knocked by through the wall behind him. She was her father's daughter and his strength had passed to her. This terrified her more than anything, why of all times, why now? She screamed loud and far at him, tears streaming down her cheeks. The cry ran hoarse as she pushed herself through her need to breathe. Just before she passed out, large arms clasped around her before she could fall to the ground. When she woke up, her father was so proud of her that everything else that had happened between them fell away and they talked for hours on all aspects of their shared power.

You late." Faye declared across to her, his deep voice thickened with the still prominent accent of his birthplace. "Your father be up in his office, and he out of patience." Instead of reaching back to the door behind him, Faye reached over to the wall on his left. With a firm push and whip of his hand, the wall sunk deep into itself, at an audible crunch, a hidden door rolled into its spot, revealing a spiral staircase.

"Why thank you good sir, your honour knows no bounds." Olivia mocked, curtsying with an imaginary dress. His stern demeanour may intimidate the tourists, Olivia thought, but she was Olivia god damn Graves, it would take more than that for her to worry. As she went to walk up to meet her father, Faye stood in front of her, pushing the palm of his hand into her shoulder.

"You be telling him tonight." He whispered into Olivia's ear, malice and contempt flowing with every syllable. Even after their first encounter, Faye had not let up on telling her about revealing the truth, although less forceful with every telling.

"I won't be doing any such thing." Olivia countered staring at him, it had been a long day and she would not put up with his threats, not today. She went through the speech she had been recited whenever Faye confronted her. This day she decided against the same routine however, and just continued walking forwards, pushing him aside with ease.

"Stupid girl." He snubbed her under his breath as she walked up the stairs.

Since the dojo had opened, the place had stayed that way twenty-four seven, with only public holidays being the acceptation. Olivia had got there close to midnight and so there was only eight fighters training. She looked down at them as she walked up the stairs. Tonight, there were four boxers, sparring in pairs. The others were two Pyromancers and two Hydrokinetics, having their own version of a snowball fight. This made Olivia stop at the balcony that overlooked the entire dojo and watch. As far as she could tell, the Pyromancers were winning. This was due to the heat of the building, confining the Hydrokinesis control to the free-flowing water from several taps behind them. A constraint posed on them to teach control. Their opponents however, basked in the heat, which added their power. Olivia watched as the trainers guided their charges with the best form of attack. She had always both admired and feared them, the trainers. Each trainer wore the same, a black, cotton tracksuit with three coloured stripes down both sides signifying their speciality. They were Shadow Legion. Her father told her when she was first introduced to them. 'Our leader, Sergeant Black may have given up on our purpose, but we have not, I have not.' It was one of the few times her father would talk about the war, but Olivia was grateful for any information she could get. The shadow legion comprised of former soldiers that Dorian had pooled together, after their term of service. Believing that the war does not stop at the border, he formed them into an organised defence of Steelhaven citizens. Having some but little government backing, the newly founded group had to work covertly, each squad using Umbrakinesis, or darkness control to keep their operations secret. This was also how they had they became to be called the Shadow Legion. Now they worked as her father's personal guard, while the name of the group may have been lost in time. Their purpose had not. As a child, Olivia wanted to be a part of her father's honour guard, continue in the fight to keep everyone in Steelhaven safe. Her father forbade it as soon as it was mentioned and would disregard any follow up reference to the subject.

The fight underneath her was getting increasingly one sided, with the Hydrokinetics' trainer giving little advice that helped. The two Pyromancers advanced on their defeated opponents who were retreating, trying desperately to keep them at bay. Hurling streams of water with little power behind the attack, so little that their attackers simply move out the way as they continued their advance. Olivia shook her head at this and turned to continue across towards he father's office. It was in that moment, when as she turned away did the water hit her, drenching her whole right side.

"What the hell do you think you're doing?" She shouted down at the celebrating Hydrokinetics, who were gleefully jumping around in a foot of water which covered the entire floor.

"Sorry." one of them shouted back up, while the other bowed. Olivia grabbed the balcony railing in front of her and split the bar clean in two.

"You will be if this happens again." She shouted down. "Now clean this mess up!" Olivia commanded as she carried on walking. As she did so, one of those she had commanded began to pull the moisture off her clothes, not making bone dry, but enough as to make her that way within an hour or so.

"At once my lady" the Hydrokinetics' trainer reassured her as the defeated Pyromancers had already started using their power to convert the water to steam. The trainer then turned on his charges and commanded them to assist.

Olivia met her father sitting behind his wooden desk. Sitting in his dark grey suit, Olivia wondered how serious this meeting had become. In the left chair facing him was a man. He had short brown hair and a soft and calm voice. Their conversation stopped abruptly when Frank noticed his daughter. With a swing of his left arm and beckoned her to join them.

"I'm glad you were able to get here so fast Liv, I'd like to introduce you to Dean Macbay, son of the Police Captain Christof Macbay." Frank gestured for his associate to stand as he said this. He couldn't have been more than five years Olivia's senior, with a five o'clock shadow across his jaw. He smiled politely as the pair shook hands. There was something untrustworthy about the man that Olivia couldn't put her finger on. They both sat in their respective seats, with Olivia moving hers around slightly around so she could view the stranger better. "He has brought some very valuable information to my attention, something you need to hear. If you would…" Frank continued, resting back in his chair with his arms folded.

"What is this about though? I don't think my university degree in art history will do much to help, some of your other contacts would do a better job." Olivia would always slide in her degree into any conversation with her father whenever she could. He had envisioned she would take over the business when he retired. She had no interest in doing so any more, much to her father's dismay.

"It's about Ms Kimberley Sangster, I hear that she is a friend of yours…" Dean interjected. Olivia's heart sank to the floor, what did he know. From the arrogant expression plastered across his face it would seem he knew a fair amount considering. Olivia darted her father a look for a fraction of a second before returning back to him. In front of the detective was a small folder, strapped to the top of the folder by several elastic bands, was a stack of A5 paper. Pulling the bands away, the detective pulled off the top letter and passed it over to her. When she had read the letter in its entirety, she flipped it over for more, but the back was blank, she shot them both a confused look.

"I don't think you have the right person, this letter has nothing to do with either Kimmi, or anyone that she knows, not to my knowledge." She reviewed the letter's contents once more, someone named Maxwell Conroy was writing letters to Dean's father about his time in the fascist group The Omegans. While the group had been a concern since its inception, there was no connection that Olivia could see to her friend. Kimberley and her talked about pretty much everything, so she was surprised of hearing about a new friend for the first time. "I'm guessing he is friend of hers that I haven't meet yet, what is the relevance?" Olivia asked, passing the letters back to Dean.

"Maxwell Conroy is a cover for an agent covertly getting us information about the organisation. There are dozens of deep undercover agents working around the country trying to identify any influence that the Nephilim have, if any. I am a handler for only three agents for now. But they are in such deep cover that their memories, personality and even physical appearance has been altered to protect their loved ones."

"A rather small amount for the police captain's son, don't you think?" Olivia asked, getting a disapproving look from her father. Olivia was then passed the rest of letters as well as the folder underneath. While she read the letters, Dean put the information into context from letters of his own, the letters themselves were transcribed with a secret code that only Dean knew.

The first letter was from Detective Asher Lucas. He had been assigned to investigate the last remaining quarry still working, Shiny Rock. Not much had changed in terms of his personality, he was a gruff, no nonsense detective and his new persona was much the same. Floyd Gunner stood half a foot smaller than his former self, a balding part running through his previous short business cut. His facial structure had been shifted lower, to better fit his low born statue. Large mutton chops down his prominent jaw. As with the others, who had gone undercover, Asher's eyes still shown sea blue, a slight tinge of gold swimming through it. Detective Lucas' report ran the same with the others that he had sent, consisting of minor changes to the production lines and the ins and outs of new workers. Those who did work at Shiny Rock, didn't last more than a month. After his third report spouting the same information, Dean wondered if Lucas' mission should be changed.

The second letter was from Detective Michelle Barton. She had been assigned to investigate a collection of farming businesses, seeing as there wasn't much work during the autumn. This meant that Michelle, under the name of Catherine now, had to move from one farming town to another, following the work. Her physique was pretty much unchanged, apart from her short black hair was changed to long and blonde. Detective Barton's personality however was completely overhauled. As a detective, Michelle was a twin for her brother in arms and best friend, Detective Lucas. She was cold and strong, with a temper that intimidate anyone. This was changed to a light-hearted girl who welcomed anyone she met. Her report was a far more fascinating read. It told of the interchange of Drem workers and how the significant decreased in crop production. It recorded the loss of production was decreased, the more Drem were working in one company. This went hand in hand with the increase in Nephilim attacks on the workers previous places of work. Whenever a large enough group of Drem lost their jobs and were shifted off to another company. A large portion of the previous company's crops were frozen in a sudden winter. Dean flagged in his report the importance of a raid of the largest farming company to be carried out.

The last of the agent's weekly reports came from Lexa, Olivia was surprised of this. As far as she knew, Lexa had left the police force to join the army. Before she could voice this, Dean continued, he had originally clashed strongly against the directors of his department against being assigned as her handler. But they refused to change the arrangement. Dean's anger changed to amusement after Detective O'Hearn's first report. It told of how she had been assigned alongside Detective Lucas at Shiny Rock and how she had lost her job within her first month. The following reports however, Dean's frustration returned as he found Detective O'Hearn's actual assignment. Her infiltration of the Omegans began slowly at first, being held back at every turn. Her final report however, told of an important mission she had been given. A mission to find missing Drem from the tailor shop that had been all over the news a few months ago.

"This folder contains all the evidence we have to connect the other agents who are reporting similar operations that group to a worrying bigger picture. That both the Nephilim and Omegans are trying, not only trying to cut off the funding for the other group, mostly received from prominent members of the merchant guild. But also, they were gathering all the recruits they can acquire, for what purpose, we have yet to find out. Also, secondary reports hinted the two warring factors were following any person they deem a threat and taking any person for interrogation." Olivia looked over to her father to gauge his understanding, then she finally understood why she had been called. Wisps of blue, grey and green shadows washed around him, morphing into two figures standing parallel to him for small moments before shifting back to formlessness. While Olivia could see them, she knew that the detective could not. She twisted her gaze back to him to be meet by more shades standing behind the detective. "With the anniversary of Lexa's parent's death looming close. I fear that she'll subconsciously bring Maxwell to their grave and put your friend in trouble. So, we need to find her before they do." A long silence stretched between the group, the shadows continue to float around them.

"Do you think he's telling the truth?" Olivia asked her father, an angry look shot at him. "There are several inconsistencies, most of the story makes sense however…"

"Story? This isn't something I would make up, this is too important too…" Dean interjected pulling himself forward, but was suddenly pulled back into his seat by, from his perceptive, by an unknown force. The formless shadows took partial solid form. Featureless and transparent, the creatures lifted Dean effortlessly into the air and held him.

"And you just happen to bring this to us, for what reason? In the hopes that we would have a common cause, like your father and Tempest had? The Shadow Legion and the police may have been allies then. But that was before the Battle of Champions." Olivia stated, her head held high in contempt. "We are going to find out all that you know and whether you are telling the complete truth to us." She finalised, as the pair of shades carried him out of the room. Dean, realising what was happening, tried his best to fight back, but the shades held in firmly in place. He screamed and went from pleads of mercy, to threats of what will happen when his father hears what was happening. They carried him over to the door to the office, only to shift slightly to the right and move to push against the wall. As they met the flat surface, all three melted through it. Her father's gaze slowly shifted to one of the shades next to him.

"Take him back to his father and tell him what happened tonight." He ordered, the shade shifted down into a bow and vanished into the wind. He then turned to the other shade. "If he is telling the truth, we need to be ready." Frank then turned to his daughter.

"No." Olivia interjected before her father could utter a word. She pushed the folder over and leaned back in her chair. "I intermediated your meeting, but I draw the line after the double cross. I have plans tomorrow. So, if we're done here."

"No, we are not." He commanded, as Olivia knew that he would, and she knew what was going to happen. As her registered boss, he would invoke the law and she would have no choice but to do her duty, as her father's assistant. Nevertheless, she could not pass up her chance of defiance. He grabbed the folder off the table and pushed it back towards to her.

It took The Shadow Legion mere hours to establish most of the validity of the detectives' evidence. It didn't take long for Olivia to plan what needed to be done. Her first plan, of working with the police to further restrict the two factions movements, was returned with a note saying. 'Is this all you can think of?' Olivia was not disheartened by this, it had been a five-minute plan and it showed. Her second plan, to intersect the two groups funds while it was in transit and use it to fund neighbourhood projects. That got another rejection, the note saying, 'you can do better than this.' That was a little more trying, as it was close to dawn and all she wished to do was sleep. Her third and final plan, to bull rush the Omegans' headquarters, gain the Nephilim's trust and destroy them in one decisive act. This one was not going to get another rejection that time, she marched up to his office and slammed it on his desk.

"Here is the last one, I am not doing another. If it's not good enough, then you do it your damn self." Olivia spun on the spot and began to walk out. She was about to slam the door behind her when.

"Thank you, Liv, I'll read this one" Frank remarked, causing her to stop.

"You'll read this one? Are you telling me that you didn't even bother to read the others? All the time and effort I put into them was for nothing?" she asked, affronted by his candour. Her father ignored her and instead continued to read her plans. She opened her mouth to say something, closed it, opened it again, only to scoff and leave the room, slamming the door behind her.

She had gotten halfway down the hall, when she heard noises coming from her father's office, sounds of a fight. Olivia however shrugged this off. It was only when she had gotten to the top of the staircase, did she realise that the noise had not subsided like she thought it would. In fact, it had gotten louder.

"Dad? Are you okay?" Olivia asked as she re entered the office. His desk had been flipped over, its contents scattered all over the floor. The large bay window overlooking the street outside covered in a thick slab of ice. The street lamp's light fracturing through, illuminating the entire room, including the four strangers standing over her father's unconscious body. Two standing with ice spike clenched in each hand. One standing over Frank's body, they then lifted him up and on to his shoulder with relative ease. The last in the group was facing the wall, inscribing it with nine strange symbols, all connected with four hexagons all interlocked within the other.

"Get away from my father!" Olivia commanded, her voice projected and echoed around the room. She reached down to her belt buckle, which detached to be used as a brass knuckle. She slipped it off and held the golden knuckles in her right hand. The two ice soldiers turned and spun the spikes in their hands. Olivia lunged at the one closest to her, the other however quickly put an end to her attack. Quickly throwing one of their spikes, which impaled Olivia through the shoulder and against the wall behind her. She cried out in pain, the blood from her wound froze as it fell. She grasped the spike, but her grip slipped away. Her second attempt to take the spike out was stopped by another spike driving through her other shoulder. Her cries became even louder. One of the group of Nephilim soldiers walked over and stared up at her, their eyes reflecting the light from outside. They lifted a hand and rested it on Olivia's temple. Wisps of fractured images darted through her mind with such force that she passed out. The last thing she saw before she blacked out, was the Nephilim leaving through a shimmering portal, with her father.

CHAPTER THREE

Having been given little to no information about what kind of greeting she and her group would receive, Chloe followed the group full of nerves. They walked curiously down a vacant alleyway, with the recruiter for the Nephilim, leading them. The group consisted of Chloe, Darren, Sara and Matt. Although Chloe had worked with them for quite a while, she never truly felt a part of the group. The other three had been together most of their life. So, when Kate promised her a way for her a place to belong. She leapt at the chance. The others were drawn in with the idea of faith. The rest of those working in Smith and Taylor stayed with Malik. As they walked down to the end of the alley, Chloe was the first to see it, pointing it out to the rest. On the wall, high in front of them twisted a small light. The closer they got to it, the larger it became. Flowing in a spiral, the light then fractured into several smaller spheres, spreading off in opposite directions. In the spheres wake, streams of bright blue waves followed, until it spanned the entire wall. Kate, stopped in front of them and turned face each of them. "This is it, I hope you are all ready for what is to come." One of the orbs formed a bubble and swam to meet her as she reached her right hand while she explained. Chloe however, was too focused on the orb to listen. The orb smothered Kate's hand, flickering brightly for a moment before retreating to join its fellows. The orb began to swim around the rest, increasing in speed and pushing itself back into the wall. Each layer began to solidify into glass, forming cracks as the orbs push further down. Repeating waves of heat began to protrude out as the vortex swirled tightly together. All that could be seen of the other side, was a bright light. Two of Chloe's group, Sara and Matt, walked forward without hesitation. As they meet what would have been the wall, the pair vanished instantly. Darren was about to follow, when Chloe grabbed his arm to stop him. "I'm not so sure about this, what if something goes wrong?" Chloe asked him nervously. Darren reached over and gripped the top of her hand, a reassuring smile stretched across his face.

"Then it goes wrong, I'm tired of our people being held down." Darren responded confidently. "I know this is scary Clo, truly." Turning to face her, he lifted her hand away from his forearm. "Remember as to why you wanted to join, if not this then when?" While she agreed, feeling so tired of the shame that accompanied the use of her power, she didn't connect that to any right to rule. When she told Darren this, he simply shrugged, turned and walked forward and through the portal. It was her and Kate left. Kate walked calmly over to her and knelt in front of her. Chloe ran them through her hair, trying to distract herself. This was a big leap of faith, something she had never put much stock in. In her experience, people were generally out for themselves, at least Humankind were. Chloe hadn't spent much time around her own kind to make adequate assessment. Being the only Drem in both the orphanage and Aine's attire, the only lasting time amongst her people had been at Smith & Taylor. Now they were asking her to just jump in with, what she presumed to be thousands of them, each with their own power and a reluctance to assist her in any way. Closing her eyes, Chloe imagined their first reaction to her power, that of mockery, even from her friends. It would only follow suit, congratulations, you can change the colour of something. It was a rare ability for a reason, because apart from her current job, no one else would take her. Her first choice when leaving the St. Marx's orphanage, was the local art college, this hope was dashed under the guise of having no formal education. An easy ruse that she right saw through. This conclusion was confirmed by the other colleges in Steelhaven and several ones in Verthollow. So, having nowhere else to go, high priest Aurelius pulled some strings and got her the personal assistant job out the goodness of his heart. Which Chloe knew was code for, get out we don't want you here. Maybe it would be different, she thought, maybe I would finally find a place that I could home, a pipe dream she knew in her heart wouldn't come true. No matter she said or did, she would be the outcast.

"It's okay to be scared." Kate reassured, resting her hand on Chloe's shoulder. "Only a fool wouldn't be. Just remember that I will always be there to help when I can, you just have but to ask." She smiled as she stood back up and offered her hand. Chloe's nod in agreement and they both starting walking forward together. The heat was boiling, the gateway roared waves of heat with its every rotation inward. Increasing the closer they got. The glass of the portal cracked slightly under their shoes. Small mounds of smoke firing up, only to be sucked in by the vortex. The light glowed brightly in front of them, revealing nothing of what was to come, which made Chloe tighten her grip of Kate's hand. A second hand matted over hers, which Chloe smiled to herself about. Maybe, just maybe, I can trust her, she thought to herself as the pair advanced through and into the unknown.

In an instant, the vortex vanished to be replaced by towers of light. Towers that sprouted high into the air, spreading down the road in front of them. The peaks of the buildings twisting to the sky, vanishing in a sea of brightly white orbs. Stepping forward, Chloe seem to synch with the floor, sending out a pulse of sparks with every step. As they walked down the street, Kate introduced Chloe to her new surroundings.

The final stop on Chloe's tour was her new home. Situated in a high-rise building overlooking the faction's church. Every surface possessed a slight translucent quality allowing a light to wash itself through. Her new apartment had large, centralised living quarters, within the centre sat a square bay of sofas that sunk below the floor. All matted in leather seats with a wooden table in the middle. The centre of the table was cut out to allow for a large crystal to levitate through said table. It sparkled in the morning sunlight. Chloe had seen those crystals all over the new city, though she had not dragged up enough courage to ask what they were for. Opposite the Main entrance, sat a large bay window that spanned the entire wall. Walking over to it, Chloe noticed the glass floor of the balcony underfoot, allowing her to see the metropolis underneath. The view outside was scattered with similar towers, all while allowing for the church to stay in focus. Kate strolled over and stood at Chloe's side. Kate told her that she was glad that she was liking her new home. She softly spun her to the left and they walked over to the room closest to the window. Engraved in the centre of the wood, was her name. As they walked inside the room, Chloe noticed that there were only three pieces of furniture inside. A single, platformed bed, placed on the back wall. Next to that was a wooden desk with conference chair. As she followed in, Kate gave Chloe all the information she needed about her formal induction into the Nephilim. It would occur the following morning in the academy building. While she had been there before on her tour, Kate highly recommended that she got there with her flatmates, to get better accustomed to the scope of the place. She then rushed out a goodbye before leaving Chloe by herself. Moving over to her new bed, she lay back for a while. Her nerves had not relented for a moment. She had never had so much and yet so little in her life, that uncertainty unnerved her. Looking over to her left, Chloe noticed a small notch in the wall. As she walked over it inspect the damage, the notch split in two, as if it knew Chloe's intentions to reveal a hidden wardrobe, filled with her new clothes. Four sets of robes, light grey with thick wrappings around both shoulders and forearms. Two pairs of grey combat boots and several other accessories. Pinned to one of the shelves was a small hand-written note. 'Check the desk.' Turning around to the table, she noticed a large folder about her introduction to the Nephilim.

The academy building stood proud on the hill just down her street, its high walls was smothered in light. As she walked in, Chloe noted that each department connected to the main hall in a spiral. And that the whole place smelled of freshly baked apple pie and a warm summer breeze. She closed her eyes and lifted herself high with an inward breath, she was brought back quickly to the ground by her group. Matt grasped both her shoulders and lead her forward, the rest of the group following close behind. Chloe did little to fight against this as she was just enjoying the atmosphere. In the atrium sat a towering, marble stage with a large group standing ready. Meeting the large crowd in front of the stage, Chloe noticed a man standing behind a podium. His hair was firmly gelled back, and he had a pair of circular glasses balanced on the bridge of his nose. Chloe stared at the man for a while, certain that she knew him from somewhere, although she could not remember where. Even when he introduced himself, the group and what their main goals were, to bring balance and order to a whole in desperate need of it. Flanked either side of their leader was two giant bodyguards with large crystal wings spread proud of their back. Their eyes glow a bright white, partially masking some of their expressionless faces. As the leader of the Nephilim, Tiberius, continued with his explanation to their new intestates. On the training they required before being fully inducted into the Nephilim, the large group standing behind him began to orderly walk forward and jumped down and met with the crowd. The crowd was then divided into a dozen equally sized groups and led off to begin said training. Chloe's first day was a long one, she was introduced to each of her mentors as well a small exercise in power application. For her that was shooting a dome of colour above her head, for it to rain down upon numerous others in her group. In the back of her class was a small crowd of institutes gossiping amongst themselves, pointing their fingers over at Chloe and laughing. Her mentor, Professor Swam, blasted a stream of lighting at them which struck the concrete wall behind. They were then sent out and told to wait outside until the class was done. Chloe felt shame because of this, thinking it was her fault that it happened. Sara, who was also in her group, sensed her discomfort and reassured her. Just childish kids, being childish kids, she said, which cheered Chloe up slightly. After the class on power management, the following classes were devoted to philosophy. What is the best application for their powers, what is the separation between Humankind and Drem, why are those with power subjugated and the history behind it, were a small amount of the vast number of subjects covered over half a dozen different classes. The last of the classes for the day were basic literary and numeracy lessons.

At the end of the day, Chloe returned to her apartment with every intention of going straight to sleep as she was tired after the long day. When she got inside however, she was met by all her flatmates, who beckoned her over to join them on the sofa in front of her. They all took it in turns, talking about their first day. Matt had been instructed on the proper way to hold his crystals in his hands and that with enough instruction, he could join the highest ranks of the Archangels. Darren smiled broadly as he told his story, of how his empowered agility and endurance was put to the test with an aerobatic training routine that pushed passed his limit, then demanded more. While they talked, Chloe sat with her legs crossed, sub consciously flexing her power. Small waves of colour beamed up into the air, evaporating into the air by a different colour entirely. Blue, green, orange and white pulses shot from her hands; becoming more frequent when it was her time to speak. No one seemed to notice, in fact, those who had material abilities joined with her. Matt forearms sprouted small crystal and Sara played with a small wisp of energy, twirling it smoothly around her fingers. Darren on the other hand had no outward tick that could be seen, not unless he got up to get something. When he went to go to the bathroom during Matt expressing his opinion on the numerous philosophy classes, he politely excused himself, grabbed the back of his seat with one hand and pulled himself up into a handstand before twisting over completely to land on his feet. The group talked for so long that only the bell to signify another day of training brought them out of their conversations. Even though they had been up all the night, they had more energy now than when the day started.

Most of Chloe's days continued like this with slight changes. Breakfast, of which comprised of porridge and water, the first two of her classes, lunch, then a further five more classes before then end of the training day. To which, Chloe would either return home or to Professor Swan for more instruction. Over time, Chloe's power grew, allowing her to construct and control all manner of colours and the different shades in between. This did not seem to impress the small group in the back however, who would still natter amongst themselves whenever it was Chloe's turn to perform. With Professor Swan doing little but throwing them out of class. After the first week had past, Chloe had had enough, just as she was to step away from the training circle in the centre of the room. Chloe spun on the spot towards the small mocking group and blast a pure white light at them. This blinded several of the group and put Chloe in detention. Which consisted of far harsher training than she could cope with. At one point she had several broken ribs, one shattered forearm and a dislodged right shoulder. Thankfully neither her injuries or those from the group were permanent. Former members of the Nekrüm, the medical corps of Steelhaven's military, had joined the Nephilim when the war ended. The Nekrüm's robes were different. Jet black, with an overhanging hood in place of the wrappings around their shoulders. While she was being healed, Chloe couldn't help but look under her healer's hood. From what Chloe could guess he could be around eighty years old, his eyes shown a violent shade of dark blue, with his milky white skin augmented by the wrinkles across his slender face. In trying to make the situation feel less awkward, Chloe asked how long he had been in the Nephilim. He did not

reply. After several move attempts to strike up a conversation, the Nekrüm turned to her, his gaze hard and unfeeling. At that moment, the warm sensation of his healing power, ran ice cold. She tried to open her mouth to apologise but her body had become unable to move. The moments of her healing, ran for what seemed like hours, the Nekrüm's stare unwavering. The moment her wounds were healed, he was gone in a flash. Chloe laid there for half an hour before she could move again. This was also the day that she noticed something.
While she knew that she and her friends had been there a while, she guessed it could not had been more than a few months. On returning to home however, seeing her reflection in the bathroom mirror, did she realised the change. When she had joined, Chloe had been fourteen years old, but the reflection looking back at her was closer to her early twenties. When she went to confer this with her flatmates, they had also aged several years of the past three months at the most. Not only that, but they seemed not to have noticed this change either. On instinct they turned towards the large crystal floating in the middle of the room. Their reflections unnerved them, and they screamed in unison. It was Matt's idea to try and find Kate, their recruiter, surely, she could explain was happening. Just as they walked towards the door to leave, there she was standing in front of them and she hadn't aged a day. They all frantically asked what was happening, with Matt's voice being the loudest. As their recruiter began to answer their questions, all sound ceased from their mouths, not for lack of trying. Kate waited for them to calm down and after she explained. She explained that, the place they were staying acted more like an altered dimension. For their training to be completed, certain things had to be put in place, one of which being a slight acceleration in time. This caused an eruption of anger from the now twenty odd-year olds, which lasted nothing more than a few seconds, before their voices were taken away again. This had been a confrontation that she was ready for, as she explained that the time shift was a small price to pay, reciting an account of the

first institutes being trained at normal speed, only for them to be woefully unprepared when an Omegan attack that killed all with little resistance. While she understood their disgust at being lied to and agreeing that they probably wouldn't have joined at all if they knew of the shift in time. She also explained that if not the change, that many would have been casualties, most fatal, in the constant bombardment of Omegan raids. The next couple of days, or what Chloe perceived as days, compounded Kate's confessions. And in the months to come, new recruits would arrive and join her group, their focus and control over their powers was laughable to say the least. It also put those who mocked her into perspective as well. Over time, she and the group even reconciled their differences.

Two months passed and Matt was the first of their group to ascend into the second tier of initiates. Followed closely by Sara. This led them to staying longer at the academy and spending most of their free time at the cathedral. While Darren could not wait to join them, Chloe wasn't so sure. The pair had lost the vigour that they once had, Chloe assumed the reason for this was because they spent less time in front of the floating crystal. When she could get all four of them together to talk, the glow of the crystal restored some of their energy, changing them from husks back to their normal selves, at least for a time. Thankfully both her and Darren joined their friends in the second tier at the same time, all his enthusiasm disappeared within this first week and as the time passed, the group meetings became less frequent. One morning they were all called into see one of the senior officers. He was short with a business cut of blonde hair and a grim expression on his face. He waited for the four to sit down before he did the same. His voice was loud and confident as he gave them an important mission. They need to get some critical information from a young woman, whom the Nephilim scouts had brought in. The officer passed over all the intelligence they had on her as well as what they needed to find.

The interior of the interrogation room was the first place Chloe had seen, that had lost its glow. The woman prisoner, was asleep on the floor with her back to the door. As Chloe and her comrades walking into the room, the door closed behind them and with it, the warmth from outside. Thousands of small spheres of light shown down from above, still barely keeping everything in the room visible. Matt walked forward and addressed their prisoner, asking, no demanding that she stand up. His tone was forceful but calm. While the rest of the group shivered because of the cold, Matt was calm, the reason for this wasn't apparent until he stepped into better lighting did Chloe could see why. Over his skin was a thin layer or crystal, sparkling and shinning the light across the room. As she got closer, Chloe could feel the heat radiating off him. In a sudden twist, Matt spun around and barked orders at Sara and Darren, to get her up, ignoring Chloe's shock. The light from above shown out a dark message, while there was no obvious signs of injury, her eyes shown dull and lifeless. Only the movement of her chest, signified that she was in fact alive. Her skin was a light grey and her hair shown a washed-out toffee blonde. Walking closer, Chloe couldn't help but notice the vacant expression in the woman's eyes. Ignoring Matt's command to ask about their target, showing the prisoner a picture, Chloe instead asked whether there was any point in even attempting it. It was clear to at least Chloe, that the prisoner was in no fit state to answer anything. Chloe would have been surprised if the prisoner even knew where they were. While Chloe got Darren to agree with her, it was clear that being in charge had gone to Matt's head, he turned sharply on Chloe and told her to watch her tone. After which, he turned and charged Sara with asking the questions, with Chloe just to show the picture instead. Not wanting to get barked at, Darren chimed in with the only other piece of information they had, that their target was an Omegan operative. The questions were repeatedly demanded by Matt at first, loud and strong, with an anger that the rest had not seen. Then Sara joined in, sending fractural shock waves down the prisoner's arm. Darren became even more forceful than that, tightening his grip on the prisoner's other arm and shouting louder. Chloe felt the hate wash through her and in an instant changed from a helpless bystander to an active aggressor. Dropping the picture as she walked forward, she began to shoot sparks of colour from her hands. Just as she was about to reach out and grab the prisoner, the interrogation room door blasted open, light blasted through. An unknown forced grasped Chloe by the waist, lifted her off the ground and dragged her outside. Her squad mates quickly following her in the same manner. Matt drove himself on to his feet, but before he could say one word. The interrogation room door had vanished back into the wall.

As the years passed and neither Chloe, not her friends, got another assignment. Age had caught up to her and the once youthful girl that had when joining the Nephilim all those years ago, was replaced by a rusted old woman who had all the power she ever wanted and yet so little time to use it. It began with a cold, just a sniffle here and there, it soon grew into a heavy weight on her chest. Soon, she could not walk and that was when she was taken to the hospital. This was it, she though, she would not get to experience the freedom and joy of being power without registrant. As she was wheeled into her private quarters in the hospital however, instead of a bed there was a woman kneeling in the middle of the room. If Chloe had known her before, her mind had ripped that memory away. The woman was chained to the floor by frozen shackles, as she moved closer, Chloe could hear a faint chant. It became louder the closer she got, until, at the precipice the noise became unbearable and she reached out and covered her ears. As she did, a spark of memory came back to her and she remembered who this woman was. Her name was Isabelle Fountas, she and Chloe had worked at her Aine's attire together. On her day Isabelle was on her, taking away every customer Chloe would try and interact with. Sometimes even going as far as leaving her to do all the work before swooping in a taking the sale at the cash register, which none of the other employees found issue with. She would demean her whenever she could and instructed the others to do the same. With every insult, Chloe retreated further into herself. Only when she was fired for simply doing her job, did she slowly regain her self-worth again.

Chloe stared down at Isabelle with contempt, if this was going to be her final act, she would not waste it. Ignoring the woman's pleads for mercy, Chloe rammed the palms of her hands over Isabelle's eyes and poured all the hate she could muster. Short waves of intense colours flowed down Chloe's arms, into her hands and through Isabelle's entire being. Every shade of colour that she could think of rushed through, quickening in frequency with the pressure. Isabelle began to shake from the trauma, but Chloe didn't care, she simply shouted at her face. She hated her, hated her more than she had ever hated anyone. She was her enemy, her and everyone like her. Looking down at her power like a curse instead of a gift, making her believe the same, forcing her to hide that part of herself. Not any more, Chloe would make sure that Isabelle knew real shame. The shades of colours had shoot through Chloe's arms had turned pure white. With one final push, Chloe slammed her hand sharply forward, creating a blast of light that filled the entire room.

When she opened her eyes, Chloe saw that she was in a large, octagon shaped room. She was standing on a raised platform in the centre and she was…young. Back to the age of when she first joined. Surrounding her, were rows of raised seats, housing all the students who had been at the academy with her, they were cheering proudly. Chloe lifted her arms high in the air and continued the white light high above her. A broad smile on her face, bright and complete, with her white eyes beaming with pride.

CHAPTER FOUR

Ever since the attack in her father's office, Olivia had refused to go home. There had to be something that gave any indication on where her father was being kept and she would not leave until it was found. Within the first few days, she had turned the room upside down, even going to the extreme of ripping up floor boards or tearing holes in the walls. But she found nothing. Sleep deprivation would take over every other day, causing her to collapse wherever she was, which was sitting next to her father's office desk most of the time. When she did, Olivia's mind brought forth a foreign landscape. A broken forest of indigo Birch trees, towering over her like giants with a slight opening amongst them, showering down moonlight. As with the other times when she attempted to move, it ended in failure. All she could do was spin on the spot, revealing yet more forest as well as out of focus objects off in the distance. Her latest stay in her dreamscape was interrupted by one of the few that trained at the gym. "I told you that I did not wished to be disturbed, now get out!" she screamed at the teenage boy causing him to run out the office. Rumours of Olivia's erratic behaviour swept through the gym quickly, but this did not detour her in the slightest. The past few days, she descended further into her obsession, focusing solely on her repeating dream, convinced it held the answers. Every time Olivia woke up from her dream, she wrote down all that she could remember. Every repetition of the dream, brought more clues into focus. She wrote down any detail that she could keep a hold of. The ancient outer Steelhaven wall towered over her to her right, Made of Talgane and reinforced higher every decade, allowing for distinctive layers of the wall to stretch miles into the sky. The wall entrenched all of Steelhaven, only splitting on either side of Mount Ashford and on the southern cliff that met the Bethram sea. Few people ventured past the walls, so the position of where the forest was stayed unknown. Olivia also noted the blanket of fallen leaves at her feet, the positioning of the constellations above, the smell of the breeze and its direction. Anything that could help. She was so preoccupied with her writings that she didn't notice the formless smoke by her side, not until it pressed against her shoulder. "What have a told you about sneaking up on me like that?" Olivia spat out in shock but got no reply. The Shadow Legion were silent, speaking only to one person, Olivia's father. While they did not say a word, they did solidify their form. The soldier stood a little over five foot, with their eyes the only feature that could be seen. "Whatever." Olivia sighed, closing the book in front of her. "Is there a reason for this interruption?" She frustratingly asked as she rubbed the sleep out of her eyes. Again, the soldier gave no response. Olivia was about to send him away when she noticed the person sitting in front of her. The woman wore an oversized coat plated in bright square tiles of wool, her auburn hair curled wildly under her brown bowler hat.

"Good evening Miss Graves, I hear that you have some trouble sleeping…" The woman answered Olivia's unasked question as she rummaged through her polka dot shoulder bag. Olivia turned to confront the legionnaire who had taken upon himself to bring outside help into her business. Who had vanished. "…Wild dreams and such." The stranger continued. "It's not uncommon for stresses of running a business, to become overwhelmed at times. It's has been happening more frequently recently. I've had fourteen new clients in the past week. Not that I'm complaining, some of the more financially gifted ones seem all too eager to find answers." She joked, not looking up from her bag as she placed several thin, white candles on the table. "If I can just find the right, ah there you are." She placed a rather large tub of paste in between the lines of candles and finally looked up. Her eyes shown white with only a swirl of grey to signify which direction she was looking. At first Olivia thought the woman was blind, until she had moved off her seat a reached over the desk, picking up Olivia' notebook and began look through it.

"I'm sorry Miss?" Olivia questioned moving herself to the edge of her own seat.

"Mrs..." the woman corrected, still not looking up, "Mrs Rania Theriane."

"Mrs Theriane, I'm sorry for what you may have been told, but I do not require your help." Olivia instructed, grabbing her notebook out of the woman's hands. "Nor did I even invite you into my office. I am very busy, so if you wouldn't mind…" She lifted her arm and indicate the door.

"From what I can tell, your experiences aren't too much different from the others who have requested my assistance." Mrs Theriane continued, not hearing Olivia's request.

"But I never asked, wait… who are these others?" Olivia questioned, fighting against her sudden need to sleep.

"I'm afraid so, most have lost someone dearest to them. Yours is your father I hear, a tragedy." Out of her bag, she pulls out a small notebook of her own. As soon as she recited her other client's experiences, Olivia dropped into a quick and sudden sleep, this did not deter Mrs Theriane, as she continued to read aloud.

The dream forest seemed clearer than before, the dull indigo of the leaves overhead shown with a brightness that was almost blinding. As Olivia reached out and ran some of them through her fingers, she realised something. She had moved from her fixed spot. Smiling at this realisation, she turned around and towards where she could remember seeing Steelhaven's wall and began to run. With every tree that she brushed past or every root she climbed over, she drove herself forward. Finding the wall would give her a better understanding as to where she was, she had to find her father, no matter the cost. She ran passed her cramp, willing herself forward. It was then, as though from behind her left ear, a voice began to whisper. "Wall, sky, castle, lake." It repeated these phases continuously, becoming louder the longer Olivia ran. She pushed herself past her limit but got nowhere. She was exhausted, she had to stop and when she did, she falling to her knees, a gust of wind and leaves encircled her. The voice increased in volume, overruling the sound of the now hurricane winds around her. Olivia covered her ears to block out the sound, but it did not work. Standing up, she tried to run through the gale, only to be dragged off her feet and twisted along with it. She flew limply in the air. No matter how hard she tried, she couldn't keep her eyes open to see anything, not even to see how high she was going. All that she knew, was that the fall would kill her from the height she was already at, and yet she was being pulled further. Higher and higher she flew, not knowing if she would ever come down, she began to feel the cold grow. Just at the peak of when began to gasp for air, the cyclone suddenly vanished. This shocked her into opening her eyes. In that spilt second before she began to plummet to the ground. She was overlooking all Steelhaven. "Wall, sky, castle, lake." The voice said one last time. This pulled Olivia's eyes to directly underneath her and she knew where to go. On the outskirts of the western Steelhaven boarder was a location only a handful of people had dared to go. The world's eye, a mile wide, marquise shaped lake. In its depths, across the sides of what seemed like an endless abyss were diamonds. All varied in size and colour, but they all shown with a twisted glow. Olivia stared at her destination as she fell, not wavering, even as it fell out of her vision. She hit the ground with such force, that it woke her up. Springing her head up, it took a while to remember where she was. When she finally did, and who had put her in such a state. Mrs Theriane had gone, and in her place, was a small note with a pair of wings stamped into the wave seal in its centre.

While walking to the meeting point, surrounded by her Shadow Legion, Olivia stared passively up at the night sky, finding comfort in the familiar constellations above. Her guard slowing their pace to match hers whenever she began to drag her feet. Unlike her troops, Olivia hadn't seen real combat and was in no hurry to experience the reality. If she had it her way, her Legion would have gone to the meeting without her. The Nephilim's invite however, explicitly requested her presence. As she noted a shooting star spiral overhead, the soldier to her right nudged her and pointed ahead for her. The forest trickled away to reveal not only the World's eye but also their adversary, ready and able, with a large domed shield guarding them. Hundreds upon hundreds of warriors stood in regimental formation at the centre of the lake, all encircling a mile-high tower that overlooked them all. Each regiment consisted largely of Cyromancers, bouncing sharply on the spot, ready to fight. Standing in the commanding position of each regiment, stood the primary symbol of the Nephilim. Smothered in plate armour and equipped with a golden spear, stood the archangels. Large, crystal wings sprouted proudly across shoulder blades with that same crystal encasing their helm, leaving only the slit in their visor uncovered. While Olivia has had no personal experience with them, her legionnaires have; and the stories told of one pure fact. When the 'archangels' were seen on the battlefield, little would be left alive afterwards. Standing behind scores of the battalions were golems of crystal and stone. Towering over ten-foot-tall and twice as wide, with two sets of arms and in place of their face was housed a large crystal, spiking high above their stature. A small group stood on the peak of the tower, just out of sight. Following it down to the ground, Olivia noticed that the water underneath her enemy was frozen solid, abruptly stopping around their boarders. Olivia stepped slightly forward, she lifted her arm and signalled to her legionnaires to stay put, refusing to advance forward and leave the safety of the forest. "We should go over the plan again," she commanded the legion commander, Hermus, who she knew had morphed to her side without needing to look. "It is a more hostile than we anticipated." Olivia lifted her left hand to hold up the collar of her fur lined coat to protect herself from a sudden gust of wind that startled her into believing they had already been spotted. This shock subsided when she noted that none of the Nephilim moved. She took a deep sigh of relief, that froze in the air.

"We split our forces into thirds…" Hermus hissed with the air, low and quiet. "Taking the first third with us, the second staying at this spot. Allowing for reinforcement if required. The final third will retreat back and around to the castle overlooking us." He shifted his arm up and point over to derelict stone keep on top of the hill overlooking the world's eye, overwhelmed with white birch trees, vines and covered in thick layer of fog. "I'll go form the squads, my lady."

"It would be best to send our strongest soldiers over to the castle, we don't know if our enemy have had the same idea." Olivia put in as Hermus went to instruct their troops.

"Of course, my lady." Hermus replied with a slight bow.

As her troops shifted into their teams, Olivia watched her enemy, wanting to find a weakness in their defences. But there were none. As she gazed back up to what she guessed was the Nephilim leadership, a loud battle horn rang out from across the far-left shore of the lake, piercing the night's silence. "What is it my lady?" Hermus asked as he returned to Olivia. Her respond was eclipsed by a second blast, louder than the first. As the horn faded away, a low and steady drumming began. Quietly at first, repeatedly flourishing throughout. The Nephilim responded to this also, moving two regiments over to greet them. The water freezing underfoot as they ventured out. Hermes spun his torso around, leaving their legs facing ahead and signalled for the legion to split while the enemy was distracted. When he turned back around, he saw that Olivia had left their secure spot and begun to stride forward to meet the Nephilim. Hermus lifted his head and cried an echoed hiss to his squad to follow. As soon as they walked out of the refuge of the forest, their smoky appearance solidified into glass. Shining black with that same dark purple smoke encased inside.

The snow under her feet shifted sharply off the ground as Olivia strode powerfully towards the shore. "Hey!" She shouted, waving her hand over her head. "Sorry to interrupt, but you better deal with us first. We would have gotten here sooner, but this place is a bitch to find. I'm not sure why we couldn't do this in some place with a little bit of heat. Out of all the places, why here? It's far too cold." Olivia slammed her feet down when reaching the shoreline, the snow propelled forward and went off into the wind. "So, are you going to come meet us or do I have to swim over?" Olivia shouted over. After a moment, frustrated that she had gotten no response and ignoring her legionnaires that had joined her at the shore. "Am I not being loud enough?" Olivia continued to herself.

"Deven'ra herself could hear you, I think that…" interjected Hermus, who stood on her right.

"Hey!" Olivia screamed over Hermus' response, projecting her voice so loud, that it echoed back to her. A sudden frost rushed through the ground and into Olivia, looking down she saw that the surface of the water in front of her had begun to freeze over. Ignoring her shiver, she carefully placed a foot onto the newly formed ground. As she did, the ice propelled itself ahead, beaconing her to follow. She let out the breath that she had been holding in, signalling again as she walked forward for her legionnaires to follow, which they did. Although she felt her anxiety grow the closer she got to her enemy, she ignored it. Strength was needed here, not cowardice. Quickening his pace to catch up with Olivia, Hermus grasped her wrist and slowed her down.

"Careful my lady, I want to get your father back as much as you do. But be cautious, we don't know the full extent of this situation." He whispered to Olivia, she reluctantly nodded back in agreement. Getting close to the Nephilim's shield, heat could be felt rushing from it, causing Olivia to take a few to take several steps back. A piercingly loud noise shattered high above them. Wincing as she looked up, Olivia watched as the ice tower started to descend. Olivia's fear took control her, pushing her back slowly through he companions, never taking her eyes off the threat. 'Why can't things be easy?' She wished to herself. Feeling somewhat safer now that her troops were a defensive line in front of her. Olivia stopped for a moment, but as her hand fell away from the revolver strapped to her thigh, she felt a something standing behind her. Spinning on the spot, Olivia grabbed her side arm on instinct. As she brought it up to protect herself, it smashed against, nothing. The gun fractured and fell to the ground, collecting in a small pile against the unseen force. "We have an issue here." Olivia commanded.

"What is it my lady?" Hermus questioned, not taking his gaze away from the tower.

"I'm not sure, be ready" Olivia responded as she shook the pain from her hand and reached out to meet this new problem. It was warm to the touch, so much so that it caused Olivia to pull her hand back. This interaction however, caused a ripple in front of her, she could feel this barrier follow her hand for a moment. At this, Olivia knew what it was. "Telekinesis," She declared to herself.

"What is it my lady?" Hermus asked again, stepping slightly forward to protect the group.

"They have one or perhaps more telekinetic in their midst, my guess is to stop us from retreating. Keep to the plan." Olivia responded, trying to stay calm. She turned back around and pressed her back against this barrier. The far-off drumming grew with every passing moment. Olivia wondered how this barrier would affect them. Slowly, she began to walk to her right, trying to find where the barrier ended so they had a chance of escaping. In trying this, Olivia saw a shimmer of light in the corner of her eye. Looking over to the source, Olivia saw another large group, whom had used the same tactic to get across. A plethora of different armoured soldiers, covered in the finest quality Talgane reinforced chain mail that money could buy. In their hands shown military grade plasma rifles, glittering brightly in the moonlight. As Olivia focused more closely on the individuals within this new group, she watched as dozens of smaller factions marched forward. All separated by their own company crest, which were housed in the centre of their chests or plastered across a tower shield, some of which Olivia recognised. The red eagle of the Endraths, the white bear of the Kaladrum, and the black hand of the Gren, were just a few of many marching in unison. They were all part of the Merchants Guild, the old power of Steelhaven. Some of their people must have been taken as well, she judged. Which only compounded the issue. More nerves shot through Olivia as she realised, they were the smallest group in the conference. When this new group met with their side of the protective shield, the drumming from the left stopped abruptly. Looking over, Olivia's suspicions were confirmed. From the shore of the lake, outstretching as far as the eye could see, were the Omegans. Crimson tinged armour, primal and powerful shined bright in the night, the whole western shore seemed to be alive with fire. At the front of the army stood a group of horsed commanders. Holding lances in their right hand, bringing them up in unison to meet the two Nephilim regiments that had finally met them. Their booming commands were dragged and distorted into the wind, as one of the archangels stepped forward. A booming laugh echoed from above. Olivia looked up and watched as the descending tower slowly revealed the Nephilim leadership. Encircled by several archangels were a group of five, all thoughts of Olivia's plan vanished from her mind in an instant. Past the giant of a man made of ice and the slender woman of stone, past the elderly man encased in a shining green mist. Standing next to the man leading the laugher was her hero and former leader of the Shadow Legion. Sergeant Dorian Black. Dressed in his old military black trench coat. This coupled with a large hood that covered much of his face. Many would not recognise him as the hero of Steelhaven, but Olivia knew better. Their eyes met, and in that instant Olivia's breathe caught in the back of throat. Her knees buckled sharply but she was able to stay standing. One of the legionnaires closest to Olivia rushed to her side. "We're in trouble, go tell your commander to speed things up." Olivia ordered the soldier in that moment, she couldn't for the life of her remember what the plan was, no matter how hard she tried. But she knew Hermus, he would be more focused on the threat around him and she wanted to keep it that way. She knew it was more than being caught off guard, something had scattered her thoughts, and this could not happen to any one of them. Upon receiving his orders, Hermus directed his team to reform to protect him and Olivia on all three fronts. Meeting with his commander, Hermus reached out and supported her by holding onto the back of her shoulder. As he did this, he secretly passed Olivia another firearm without the chance of anyone seeing. She nodded thankfully to him and looked over to the man next to Dorian, whom she guessed was the leader of this meeting. For some unknown reason, Olivia could recognise his face and, yet she knew they had never met. She knew nothing about the man and yet felt as though she had known him her entire life. Unlike his companions, who wore the power on his sleeve. He wore a white suit with golden thread, his hands were outstretched in front of him and resting on white staff, waist height and tipped with a giant red figure.

"Welcome!" he boomed loudly over the lake, bringing his cane to one side and walking forward. "My name is Tiberius." He paused for a spell before continuing. "I am grateful to see that my invitations were well received, although I was not expecting such a convoy." He turned to his right, where Dorian was standing, and spoke something to him. Dorian acknowledged his request and waved his hands in a circular motion in front of him, his palms facing the groups on either shore. For a moment nothing happened, that was until an Omegan soldier tried to walk forward, to shout up to the tower. When it hit him, and the soldier crashed to the ground. Shock spread across his compatriots as they charged forward, only to be met by that same force. Their leadership spun around and saw, to their horror, that all but a third of their forces had been blocked away from them, leaving them severely outnumbered. One of them spurred his horse forward, pushing through their welcoming party and charging the enemy. Stopping his horse between the two factions, his lifted up his lance, the tip of which had shifted aside to the reveal the barrel of a gun. Before he could utter a word however, one of the Nephilim soldiers rushed forward and launched an attack on the man. Piercing his shoulder with a spike of ice and slamming him to the ground. The leader screamed out in pain as his horse bucked and bolted away. Olivia watched as the horse met the northern shore and to her surprise, the horse was able to safely retreat. As she brought her focus back to the matter at hand, she watched. In retaliation to their commander's injury, the Omegans pushed harder against what Olivia now knew to be Dorian, to no avail. "I told you to bring only a small company with you, no more than that what was required, one gross I believe was my exact phrasing." Tiberius clarified to them, looking over to the Merchant guild's party to see that they had found the forcefield also. "It is good to see that some of you can understand orders." Tiberius smiled down at Olivia and her Legion, who stood not even a quarter of that number. This smile however, was quickly dropped when Olivia walked forward to respond.

"This does not seem like a fair trade, you have three, if not four times that amount and surrounded by a shield of your own. How do you expect us to trust you under these circumstances?" Olivia questioned standing right behind her vanguard.

"Because we choose to." The stone commander shouted down. "Do not stand there and deny the fact that if you had the ability to defend yourself such as us, that you would not." They leaned down onto their knee and peered over the tower's edge. "You should be grateful that we are having this conversation at all."

"If that's how you really feel, then why even call this meeting at all?" Olivia shouted back in confusion.

"Because we have a serious matter to discuss." Tiberius commanded down, bringing order back to the conversation. "It has come to my attention, while we will never agree on the future of Steelhaven, we all have goals that could work with each other." Tiberius turned to face the Omegans. "Your goal for example, to remove all the Drem from Steelhaven, am I correct?" This question brought forth a roar approval. While not all could be understood, most were a variant of 'you're all dead' and 'this is our country.' Tiberius simply laughed at this and continued. Turning around to look over the Merchants. "While you just wish for things to go back to the way they were, where you had control and none of your absolutes were ever questioned." This got no response at all, the merchant's soldiers simply glowered back. "And as for you," Tiberius continued, "you would be happy to have your leader back, correct?" Olivia froze at this, not knowing what to say, in that moment she wasn't sure if he meant her father, or Dorian himself. While she wanted her father returned, she desired to have Dorian back as well. To not have that damning burden of leadership pressing down on her shoulders any more. That was something she deeply desired. "Well, we are here to grant all of your requests. Similar to all of your ambitions, we too wish for things to return to the way they were. For the balance to be restored, and I believe that we can all come to an agreement." Tiberius declared, slamming his cane into the tower floor. As the echo reverberated around, Olivia could hear the ruffling of trees coming from behind the Nephilim. Fear rushed through her again, perhaps her reinforcements had been discovered by another group and they were being pushed back to reveal their deception before the planned time. Olivia watched as this unknown addition walked through the trees. Led by a several Cyromancers, were not only her soldiers but the Omegans and merchant soldiers. It appeared that the other groups had come to the same idea and sent their own reserves up to the fort above. Their hands bound together by ice with a large iced collar around their necks and across their shoulders. The large slab towered over their heads, the weight pressing their chins onto their chest to keep them subdued. They were watched by all as they walked over to centre of the lake. When they met with the Nephilim's forcefield, to Olivia's surprise, they vanished. On instinct, Olivia walked slowly forward, signalling to her legion to stay put until called upon.

Noting that Olivia's movement, the leaders of the other groups, barring the injured Omegan general, walked in similar fashion to meet the Nephilim's prisoners. Not wanting to show fear, Olivia marched through the barrier without hesitation. It washed over her, moulding around her as she passed through. When she met the other side, the barrier seemed to cling onto her for a moment before falling back. The Nephilim soldiers had vanished, in fact everyone had vanished. Leaving only Olivia herself and the prisoners held down in the ground. The formidable tower eclipsing the moon overhead was now reduced down to a small platform, not more than a couple of feet off the ground. With a welcoming smile and outreached arms, Tiberius beaconed Olivia forward. She did so, but curiously. Hermus had prepared her for this. "They will try to pull you out of the familiar the first chance they get. Remember why you are here." Olivia remembered, nervously rubbing her hands together as she walked. 'For my father, for the grumpy old bastard.' She whispered to herself. In front of her sat her captured Shadow Legion and them alone. Pulled into the ground, dirt and stone packed over their knees, up to their waste. Although she wished to walk directly over to them, she knew better and headed over to her adversary instead. The closer she ventured towards the group, the warmer it seemed to become. Great waves of heat in fact, putting her at ease. Not the right state to be in, she knew. After trekking several miles in the blistering cold however, she could not help but be calmed. Not wanting to get too close, she stopped a few feet away from their podium and folded her arms. Secretly grabbing the pistol hidden away inside her overcoat, ready to defend herself if needed.

"Greetings my friends, while our meeting could have been arranged under better circumstances. It warms my heart to see such upstanding citizens, putting their trust in a stranger. It is a rare quality, but is always a welcoming sight." Tiberius projected loudly as he walked to the edge of his stage. As though he was talking to a large crowd. A loud gust of wind rushed passed her, silencing whatever thought that was in her head. "You see..." Tiberius continued, walking forward. The edge of the platform descending with him. "...It is with a heavy heart, that I must reveal that there stands treachery within this fellowship, even before it got off the ground." He pointed across to his bound prisoners. The silver ring on his index finger, glinting in the barrier's light. This was a welcome invitation, finally Olivia could survey the captures and find her father. Although Tiberius continued to explain. Olivia did not listen, but began to examine each of the prisoners faces instead. Her nerves spiking at every new face. There sat eight men and six women, all around similar ages and all known to her. When she finally met the last face, she shoot her gaze back. Not to Tiberius, who was still explaining, but at her former childhood hero.

"Where is my father?!" she commanded Dorian, her anger twisting her demand into a screech. Loud and forceful. This stopped Tiberius dead in his tracks.

"I'm...I'm sorry?" He questioned, flustered by the interruption. Another gust of wind passed her, pushing a strange sound into the air. Olivia took a deep breath and ignored it.

"I am here for one reason, and one reason only. For my father..." She continued, again at Dorian. Not even glancing in Tiberius's direction.

"So, you do not care what I have told you?" Tiberius continued, irritated by the respect that he was not getting. "That government agents have infiltrated your organisation, under advanced and unnatural disguises, for the sole purpose of destroying everything that you hold dear?" Olivia did not respond to this, not out of shook. In fact, this was something that she had already been brief on. By the police themselves, when she went to meet them and hatch a plan to save her father. They agreed that, all evidence that they had accumulated on both her father and his Shadow Legion, would be misplaced. In return, she would help them. This served her just fine. Just as she had done to the prisoners, Olivia examined Dorian face, hoping to find some subtle indication of what he knew. The wind blew hard around her, turning into a storm, blasting out shoots of force. Pushing Olivia back with every pass, but she didn't care. He had to know, out of everyone, he must know. As their eyes finally met, Dorian's emerald green eyes stunned her. They were dull. Duller than Olivia had ever seen them. She had known him her entire life and yet she had never seen him look so lifeless. His skin turned beyond pale, with sunken cheeks that made him look almost skeletal. Deep set bags under his eyes with a vacant look of a man that had lost all hope. Her anger dropped slowly away. Maybe the last few years had been harder on him than she thought, it had been over a decade since they had last seen each other. She tried to recall when that was but couldn't. She knew one thing, that something was off. He had been her hero for so long. Perhaps now, she was finally seeing him. Not as the vanguard of truth and justice, but as a man. A broken man. She opened her mouth to speak, but before she could utter a word. Dorian had flickered his gaze towards to direction of Tiberius and back. Instantly knowing what this meant, her gaze rolled over to him. He was angry, his calm demeanor replaced with a fury that terrified her. His eyes, wild and yet focused, piercing into her very soul. His gritted teeth snarling with every breath. Without taking his eyes of Olivia, he walked stiffly over to the prisoners. Lording himself over one and violently smacked the palm of his hand into the prisoner's forehead. In that instant, the stick thin prisoner erupted into the giant of a man that Olivia knew as her father. Large bruises around his face and torso, with a large cut across the right side of his neck, weeping blood. His eyes were pure white and the only response to seeing his daughter was a stream of drawl from the corner of his mouth.

She pushed herself to run to him, but nothing happened. She tried again and again, she could not move a muscle. "I am trying...," Tiberius stated calmly, his anger at its boiling point. "I am trying, to help!" He screamed, shutting off the storm that had massed around them in an instant. His clenched right fist lifting up and open enough for him to scratch the back of his head in frustration before thrown back to his side. "These people will stop and nothing to get what they want, nothing! Do you understand me?" Tiberius paused for a moment. Getting no response, he began to walk towards Olivia. "Of course, you don't, how would you possibly understand? You are nothing but a child. You will continue to do the same as you've always done. Conform, because that's all you know." Tiberius stood level with Olivia who was unable to do anything but plead for mercy inside her own head." He looked her up and down and scoffs. "You're worthless." He thrusts his right hand towards Olivia's forehead, all the rage and hate focused into a strike. Just as it was about to connect a sudden blast of energy and sound rained down from above them. Olivia breathed an airless sigh of relief, she was safe.

CHAPTER FIVE

The man woke up surrounded by screams, screams of hate and of death. Looking up, he saw a group of people standing in front of him, held back by some unseen force. This did not stop them from spewing what the man could only know as pure rage towards him, he could not understand a word they were saying, but he knew that wild look in their eyes. He had never met any of them in his life. Or had he? He though back of any kind of instance that would have brought on this kind of response. He could not recall a thing, not what had happened that day, that month or that year. In fact, no matter how hard he tried, he could not remember a thing. Where did he grow up, who were his parents, what was his name. All these answer had been lost in the ether. Hyperventilating at this realisation, he wished with everything that he had, to be anywhere that wasn't there. In trying to stand however, the man felt a force holding him down. Looking down, the man saw that he was sunken into the ground, as high as his waist. The ice-cold ground sent a shock of frost up his spine. He was buried however, the ice had somehow formed around him, and it was growing, as though it was slowly devouring him. A sudden scream sprang up to his right, looking over to see he was not the only one in this danger. He was entrenched by dozens of others just like him. The person next to the man was wearing the same clothes, his eyes were flush with desperation and tears. He stared, unblinking at the man. The man opened his mouth to tell him to calm down and ask what was going on. But he couldn't. He didn't know how, he knew what he wanted to say, but the word wouldn't form. He opened his mouth and to his surprise, now he was the one screaming. The man tried again, and this too resulted in another scream, louder than the first. This must have meant something to the other man, as he screamed back. Other groups around the man began to follow suit. The man was concentrating so hard to communicate with this man, that he didn't notice the sky above them shift from midnight blue to orange. Looking over at the first group in front of him, the man found them laughing. He turned his confusion over at them, it did not matter why he was there any more. There stood a group, refusing to help the dozens of people in clear need of rescue. He screamed violently towards them, again and again, until his voice gave out. He rested his head against his chest in an attempt to chase his breath. The screams around him were becoming unbearable, all he could do was focus on his breathing.

A deep inhale and held for four seconds
A longer breath outward and held for seven seconds.

A sudden blast from above silenced everyone. Opening his eyes and sprung his gaze up at the source. The man saw three shockingly bright spots of white light in a pyramid shape. He sat there mesmerised, each light having its own twinkle. Small but distinctive. The largest of the light was spending out a steady tick that only got closer. The more the man stared at them, the more they resembled, something. He knew what they were called, but again, could not translate that into words. The group in front of the man turned to face the lights. Instantly, long streams of pulses sprouted from the objects in the group's hands. Undeterred by this, the light began to whistle beam down streaks of energy. The man felt awe spread through his chest as the energy danced down to meet the group, lighting up the entire night sky. This awe turned to terror however, when the two forces came in contact with each other and the taunting group splattered into a sea of red which washed over the man, painting him in blood.

When he opened up his eyes, everything had changed. He was on his side, without any other option, he watched as masses of what he guessed were his people; considering they were in same crimson armour were gunned down with ease right in front of him. The helicopters dove across the sky from behind him, wave after wave. The man lifted his arm to cover his eyes, it never dawned on him until a few moments had passed that he was no longer constrained by the ground. He did not waste this opportunity, he watched and counted. After some time, the man noted a pattern to their assaults. He would have three minutes to run as fast as his legs would carry him. The man also noted his surroundings, that if he wanted to survive, he needed to get to the forest straight ahead of him. As soon as another wave flew over him, he began to run for his life. Whoever was attacking, they did not care if anyone got caught in the crossfire. It was a massacre. Three minutes. The man dove into the nearest crater created by one of the previous attacks. He landed face first next to what was left of a person's leg. Blasted off at the thigh with blood pouring out. Jumping away from it, the man slipping of more body parts. A dismembered head caused his hand to slip away from the ground, slamming into and crushing an already crushed in torso. The man closed his eyes tightly and focused on counting the minute that he would need to stay in place. Then he could move. When trying to get back up, the man tripped, but was able to keep his balance and continue on. The cover in front of him was getting thin, but he knew that he only needed to find some protection once more and then on the third run he would be in the safety of the forest. As he ran, the man looked all round for anything that would shield him, but he could see nothing. Two minutes-thirty. He was getting desperate, that had to be something. Looking up, the man saw flying spikes of ice shooting into the air like machine gun fire, he had seen small clumps of these attack when he first woke up but not on this scale. He didn't care whether they were friend or foe. He needed to find cover from the next wave. Still rushing through streams of dead bodies, the man finally found the source. Their uniforms were ice blue and the spike seemed to be spouting from their hands. In that moment, the man had a terrible idea, but no time to find a better solution. He ran towards the new group. The largest of the group was the first to spot him, he cried out and the rest turned to attack the man. Before they could fire a single attack against him however, the man bull-rushed his way through their ranks. Moments after, the air strike came. The group on the ground was so focused on the man, they didn't react to this and were blasted apart. The man was also caught in this attack and flown off his feet.

The man slowly opened his eyes to find a woman kneeling over him. She had hold of both of his shoulders and was desperately trying to wake him. This sight calmed him down, finally someone who knew who he was. That thought passed in a flash when he also remembered where he was. He screamed in her face, which caused her to fall back, and he got up to continue his escape. Although he was finally in the forest, the man knew that he couldn't stay there and continued on. Off in the distance, above the trees. He spotted a derelict castle. Overgrown by the forest and little in terms of any real protection. But if he could get there, he knew that he would be safe. Shouts from the woman who found him grew closer, even over the fighting off in the distance. He didn't know why she was so infatuated, but he wasn't going to stick around and find out. He sprinted through the trees, pushing against them to propel himself forward. All of a sudden, the trees vanished to reveal a stone path, which lead straight up to the castle. He smiled at his good fortune and charged up to his destination. The main gate was overgrown by encroaching trees so the only way inside was the hole through the watchtower to the right. Slowly walking through the hanging vines that covered his way. The man was greeted by a sea of fireflies, sparkling above like stars. Through the vine were trees littering the courtyard. His first step inside was onto a fallen branch, which scattered the creatures instantly. Their light gone with them in a flash; replaced by the night sky. The moment that the man's eyes met the moon, he became severely drowsy. A tiredness that followed him with every step. He pushed himself through it. Knowing that, no matter how tired he felt, he must find a safe haven. This thought slowly fell apart the more he advanced however. Until he could go no further. He pushed his back into the closest tree and lowered himself slowly to the floor. Resting his head back, he finally found some rest. If only for a moment. Through his hands, the man felt the ground tremble. This shook him awake. As he searched for any sight of the source. He noticed that things around him had changed. With every sweep in either direction, the trees were in different positions. Confused by this, the man stared directly ahead and watched.

It began slowly at first, a branch breaking of in the distance, a bird song shifting in position without any sound of its wings. A crack of the ground breaking apart, then again. Yet nothing had moved, at least nothing he could see. Whatever was out there, he knew that it would be best to meet on his feet. He pushed down on the ground, trying to make as little noise as possible while he stood up. Whomever was around him, it seemed not to have noticed as they continued their own movements. It was only when he had planted his feet back onto the ground, did everything fall deathly silent. As he shifted his weight away from the tree, a tremor rumbled through the bark. The vibration sent chills through his entire body and down into the ground. The man froze, unsure if the presence watching him would allow him to move. A whisper begun around him. A hum that was welcoming and yet terrifying. The man wanted to run and hide. Fear held him from doing anything, simply to breathe. A branch fell to rest on his left shoulder. When the man went to push it off however, it had moulded itself around his shoulder, wrapping vines across to his chest and plaited around his other arm, holding him in place. He was then lifted off the ground and spun in mid-air. The creature looked like a tree and yet wasn't. It's bark seemed to shift along with the breeze. It's branches grew out the side of it's trunk, functioning less like arms and more like tentacles. Each strand strengthening their grip around the man. The continuing vibration grew stronger, pulsing much like a heartbeat; in a rhythm of three. As the man looked around to find any way he could escape, he noticed it. A large lump up on the summit of his captor. With every pulse, the mass grew larger and features began to from. Eyes, blood red and sunken deep. Small twigs sprouted up and out to form a long wave of plaited hair. Finally, a mouth, that roared out powerful a silent screech. It pushed the man back in the creatures grip, if not being held tightly. There would be no telling how far he would have been blown away. Slowly stopping, the creature pulled their captive closer and stared, tilting it's head to examine the man closer, strands of its hair stretched towards the man's face and began to brush against it, as if it was mapping out his face. Shutting his eyes, the man trembled and pulled away the best he could. This was met with a loud screech. When he opened his eyes again, the creature's features seemed to have grown more detailed, it's eyes had changed their shape to match his and two slits where their nose would be. The creature barked several more times, trying to communicate something to the man. He tried to retreat again, to no avail. So, he had the only thing he knew how, scream. The man belted out an ear-piercing shout which echoed all around the courtyard and back, this caused the creature to pause, before belching out what sounded like laughter. The man was twisted around the creatures trunk, with its head following him around, still watching him with an unblinking stare. On the other side, the man was met by dozens of the same creatures and yet nothing alike. Large towering oaks off in the furthest corner converse amongst themselves and not taking note of what was happening. Several other seem to cowered away instead, pushing themselves into the outer wall of the fort, shedding their bark in place of hard stone. A splash of water pulled the man's gaze away from them and towards a plethora of water creatures, choosing to shift and flow with the water around, he wouldn't have even known that they were there until one of them began to step out onto the grass, their tentacle like legs folding over one another as it advanced. With each tentacle growing moss across its length. As they moved closer, the man was lowered to the ground. He was surrounded by the giants, all laughing and conferring with one another. The man tried to leave while they were distracted. However, every exit was blocked. Perhaps screaming could help again, and so he tried. With one giant intake of breath, the man belted out a second cry. All his polymorphs simply looked down in silence. He had said something rude, he felt it. Before he could scream again, the creatures erupted in further mounds of laughter. Which the man nervously joined in with. They must know him, and they were just playing a joke, that must be it, he thought. Then all of sudden, they stopped. This made the man uneasy again, so he screamed. At least he went to. Just before he could make a sound, there were dozens of vines, pebbles and threads of grass wrapped his mouth closed. Off in the distance was a shout. In all the commotion, the man had forgotten about the battle raging outside. He closed his eyes to shut out all other sounds and hear how the fight was going. Silence was all that could be heard, that and the shout. It beamed across again and the man opened his eyes, only to find that he was standing there, alone. Although he knew that he should follow suit and disappear, something inside told him to stay. Whether that be bravery, stupidity or something deeper, he could not tell. The man nervously watched as the unknown person walked through the watchtower entrance. The woman had long, curly hair that just passed her shoulders and a face that man was certain he has seen before. When she finally met his gaze, she smiled broadly, and she rushed to him. As she did, he remembered. He recoiled slightly, had she brought them to finish what they had started? He didn't get far however, as soon as she was close enough, the woman pulled him into a tight embrace. After the initial shock had faded, the man felt a wave of comfort wash over him and held her close. They stood there for a moment, forgetting everything else. The woman whispered something, he did not need to understand to feel comfort from it. She pulled away, still talking and smiling, streams of tears falling down her cheeks. He wanted so desperately to understand what she was saying. Just as before, something in the pit of his gut told him that she held all the answers. He smiled back at her and listened. They moved over to kneel beside the giant elk growing in the very centre of the courtyard. Dawn was quickly approaching, and the cold breeze had begun to wash away. None of that seemed to matter however, he was safe. It was only when the woman reached into her bag and pulled out a small necklace, did that feeling of security vanish. He stood sharply up and began to back away. His eyes fixed on the item, he lifted his hands up in defence. The confusion on her face did not help matters. She reached out again, holding the necklace in both hands. Every fibre of his being pulled him away from it. He knew what that item would bring, and he wanted no part of it. The woman quickly dropped it into her left hand and grabbed both of his with her right. She stared deep into his eyes, tears free flowing more than ever. Before he could do anything in response, the woman spoke a solitary word, that he heard.

"Please."

Then it didn't matter how he felt, he knew what he needed to do. He took a deep breath in and turned over his hands to receive the necklace. The woman nodded knowingly at this and gently place it onto the man's hands.

It happened in a flash, of a life that was not his. A life of a young girl growing up with her soldier father. Of her severe difficulty in making friends, with moving to a new school. Her need to escape her loneliness by focusing on her studies and the moment when she met the most important person in her life, Kimberly.

After that, the transfer seemed to alter, become brighter and yet continued on. Onto her graduating from Steelhaven University with a doctorate in psychology. To the love of her life's first live album release to the public and of their first day living together. After that however, everything took a sharp turn and she found herself rushing down a hospital hallway. Running faster than she ever had before and charging into the room at the end. There sat Kimberley, surrounded by healers being supervised by a single doctor. When she demanded to know what had happened, the doctor turned, without saying a word and pulled her back into the hall. Having no luck in calming her down, the doctor gently reminded her that this was causing more harm to the woman she loved. She nodded and asked to see Kimberley's injury report. To which the doctor agreed. What she read made her burst into tears and fall to the floor. The complete Loss of both of her legs, a large portion of her right arm, seventy percent of her ribs on her right side. She had also received multiple stab wounds to her neck and left shoulder. And finally the removal of surface tissue across the right side of her head.

The doctor tried to console her the best he could, but she was too distraught to listen. It was only when the healers had come out, did she even try to move from her spot. She staggered up and walked into Kimberley's room.
Her eyes were cold and lifeless, her breaths were shallow and far apart. Lexa sat next to her girlfriend and held her hand, squeezing it tight. Kimberley simply stared off into the distance. She had no idea what to do or how to help. With all her psychological knowledge and all she could do was hold her hand. Trying so desperately to find anything to say. Moments passed and Lexa did the only thing that she could think of and pulled Kimberley tightly into an embrace. This however, still got no response. Lexa tightened her grip around Kimberley and Lexa wished with all her might that she could take her pain away. It was in that moment, that her wish was granted. All of Kimberley's memories of the past twenty-four hours rushed through Lexa like a bolt of light. All her pain and fear,

concentrated into a fraction of a second. Lexa plummeted to the floor, screaming at the top of her lungs and grasping at her legs with her left hand. Kimberley swayed in her bed, the shock of the transfer throwing her out of it. It was only when she looked down and saw her girlfriend in such pain, was she able to focus and rush to Lexa's aid.

The walls of her memory fell away like glass, bringing Lexa back to both the present and her own body. Kimberley kissed her strongly and held her in that embrace. "Are you alright?" Kimberley asked, cupping Lexa's jaw with her hands. Lexa nodded and smiled slightly. Kimberley pulled her close and held her.

As her memories settled back into what felt like their original position, Lexa's eyes began to fade in the new dawns light.

THE END

Printed in Great Britain
by Amazon